The Fee

CN0040b609

Peter T Clark

Copyright © 2022 Peter T Clark

All rights reserved.

ISBN: 9798844558757

DEDICATION

To Len and Eileen Clark, who as well as being the best parents I could wish for, also gave me a love for Science Fiction and Fantasy.
We all need an escape from reality sometimes!

CONTENTS

ACKNOWLEDGMENTS

With thanks to Susan Clark for the Front Cover Design.
Thanks, too, to Sarah Hall and Olivia Daly for proof-reading.
Thanks to all three for their massive encouragement, too.

Part 1 - Coldharbour

1 THE STORM

The wind was up, just as old Garrik had warned them, but there was still plenty of time to return to Coldharbour before the approaching storm reached its peak. Being left out at sea overnight in the full force of nature's rage would be a disaster. With the tide long turned the Surge would be arriving soon, which was a relief, but that didn't make Luke any less angry with himself. He knew he should've taken note of the old man's premonitions, as he usually did.

It didn't matter that he'd been wrong for weeks. It didn't matter that they'd be living on half rations soon. What mattered was that he'd ignored his father's opinion that going to sea was a bad idea He shouldn't have been impatient and insisted on going out to fish without the permission of the Elders. He shouldn't have persuaded Olaf that it was worth sneaking their boats out in the middle of the night. With Olaf in turn talking Jarnock into joining the escapade, in the event three boats had set out in time for the Outsurge.

And now three boats were out there facing the wrathful waves, and inevitably three fathers' equal wrath would get them when they returned. Three shiploads of heavy catches wouldn't help much either, he thought wryly to himself. Even if the villagers, his father among them, tucked in and ate of the bounty his foolhardiness would ship home! And worse anger if one of the returning boats were to be lost on returning, always a possibility, since the other two skippers were less able than him. With less Feeling.

Never mind, the timing should be ok. Tight but ok. And as the most gifted it was his call to direct them in. Closing his eyes he sunk his consciousness deep into himself, deeper yet into the wood of the boat and down, down into the waters below. And there it was, the Surge coming, as he'd known it would be, even without Feeling first. His instincts were as reliable as ever. Just a shame his weather sense wasn't so well developed.

Opening his eyes he saw Jarnock and Olaf looking and awaiting his signal, and without hesitation he waved his arm forward. Instantly the other two boats whipped round to catch the wind and sail towards the currently invisible harbour entrance. No-one who didn't know it was there would ever think that the Cleft Rock hid a gap large enough to admit the boats of Coldharbour. One after another the three smacks passed the Cleft Rock and then, powered by the wind funnelling in behind, they whipped their tillers smartly to spin the boats sharp left past the entrance rock. Quickly, almost automatically at this point, the young men latched their tillers, rapidly released their up hauls and dragged the sails down. Winds were fluky in the corridor and had in years past driven boats onto the sharp rocks lying on both sides. The trick was to allow the momentum already gained to keep the vessels straight until the Surge arrived.

Usually with twenty or so boats coming in together, as was more normally the case, the priority was to get the sail down as quickly as possible and then get back to the tiller to concentrate on avoiding other boats and the rocks. But with just the other two, the fishers had time to fold and stow their sails.

Stoically, Luke thought it would save him having to return to the vessel after his father had bawled him out! Though with the rain hitting at that moment there were more pressing concerns. Stormy conditions made the currents more uncertain, more unpredictable. More dangerous.

Then again, the other advantage of fewer boats was that Luke had been able to take a later opportunity to pass the Cleft Rock and, not far behind the rain, came the Surge.

Not much more than a routine tidal rising that hit the whole of the coast in this locality. However, the idiosyncrasy of the entrance to Coldharbour made the Surge the key to entering the harbour where Luke and his community lived. A hidden, virtually tideless lake, formed millennia ago in a volcanic crater, with but one way in - a winding and shallow channel bound by sheer sides and, below the water line, sharp rocks that would rip the hull off a normal boat, with or without the Surge. Hence Luke's boat, with its peculiarly shallow draught and lifting keel.

How folk had first discovered the secret haven that was Coldharbour, no-one was entirely sure. Luke imagined an ancient forebear whose natural level of Feeling had led him to stumble upon the entrance just as the Surge and the pure blind luck to navigate the Curve had coincided. But the culture of never talking of the past had meant he had never explored his theory with anyone. Training however was vital, and though Luke was fortunate to have particularly high levels of Feeling, he somehow doubted if anyone could navigate such complex manoeuvres without the addition of generations of experience.

Nevertheless, someone had to have discovered the technique first. And having discovered the way in, together with the additional delights inside, one could only assume he went out and brought others to settle the land within.

No point though in looking back now for, as one of the current generation of inhabitants, Luke had no time to consider the heritage and roots of Coldharbour. He could Feel the Surge coming behind him long before the boat began to pick up momentum once more and started to buck and weave. Guiding with the light touch of the experienced sailor, he steered it forwards and aimed for the middle of the channel and the entrance to the Curve. The water around the corner was barely inches deep most of the day. Only when the Surge arrived was it passable. And then only with Feeling.

Luke waved briefly to Olaf and Jarnock in their boats as they came alongside, for there was room for up to four of the narrow craft, and then did what no normal sailor about to sail through a thin perilous channel would dare. He shut his eyes. As did the other two skippers. They breathed gently, calmly filled their minds with Feeling, just as the Surge hit.

The three small craft lifted and shot through the Curve, scant inches above the tooth-like rocks below, steered by tillers, but led by nothing more than the mystery nobody understood, but all of Coldharbour depended upon. Right, left and then right again, the impassible Curve was navigated as boats bucked and twisted and finally shot through the Spires - twin rocks that marked the entrance to Coldharbour, just as the Cleft Rock marked the start of the canal.

Exhilarated as always by the rush of the Surge and the joyfulness of Feeling, Luke opened his eyes and, roaring with laughter, cracked the keel back down and steered for shore. He had his father to face down yet, but with the Curve safely navigated, the storm barely started, the boat intact and a healthy haul of fish he felt pretty sure that parental wrath could be dealt with.

If only he'd looked behind him, he would not have been so confident.

2 OUTLANDER

Luke felt the bow gently run into the sand and calmly and cooly stepped off the boat, knowing that all around him hands would pull in his boat and lash it to the mooring stake. That's what the folk did when the fishing boats came in. His skills lay in controlling it on the water and he left the menial task of making safe his vessel to others. Besides he had a bigger fish to fry as he sought to face off his father, Arlaf, though he was pleased to see Marsha's admiring glance out of the corner of his eye. Impressing her more, though would have to wait until he'd been lambasted by his father, as inevitably he would be.

The key, he'd decided, was to meet Arlaf's eyes and not be intimidated by the power in the Elder's stare. Meet the eyes and not blink. Even as the heat of the inevitable vitriol poured from his lips, the goal was not to flinch, not to quail and yet at the same time ensure the expression he held was neither cocky nor insolent. Surprisingly, however, the stream of condemnation was not forthcoming and as Luke walked purposefully up to face the glare, he found his father's eyes appeared almost to be looking beyond him.

Nevertheless, he started on his prepared speech, in which he would abase himself but ultimately hope the safe return of all boats, with holds full of fish, would ameliorate any punishment. The prospect of full bellies would reduce it by some weeks, surely? And he could use the time ashore to find different ways of impressing Marsha. But as he'd hardly started, "Father, I did wrong and I ..." he realised that Arlaf's eyes really were looking past him. Over his shoulders in fact. His words grinding to a halt, he stopped, turned and followed the direction of the eyes of his father and indeed of the whole community.

There, In the middle of Coldharbour crater, was a sail. Quickly checking that Olaf and Jarnock's boats had also moored, he stammered uncertainly.

"Who the hell else came out? I never saw anyone else. I checked. I looked behind before we passed the Cleft Rock. I know it was dark with the storm approaching but I'm sure I would've seen if ..." And again his words ran out.

"But you never used Feeling behind you, did you?" spat out his father. More a statement than a question.

"But I did, I always do. I..." he started uncertainly.

"Never mind that," cut in Arlaf. "The bloody fool's got no idea of riding the Surge to shore. He's putting his sails up and tacking in. We'd better get these blasted fish in right now. We'll have plenty of time to do that by the look of his technique. Probably have time to gut and salt them too. Not to mention hold an Elders' Session and decide what to do with him when he lands. Plus agree a punishment for the fool who led him in Oh son, couldn't you have used your brain, your eyes or even your Feeling for a change? The village expects more from the son of an Elder. I expected it too."

"But ..."

"No buts, just get the damn fish in. And don't expect me to be impressed by the size of your haul."

Luke shrugged and turned to oversee the landing of his catch, secretly rather pleased his father had noticed its size. With disaster tacking in from the crater, it was good to have something positive!

Meanwhile, out in the water, Aldred was too busy with his manoeuvres to consider positives or negatives. Having stolen the boat and managed to escape from his pursuers, he had imagined he would sail up the coast and land after a few miles. But hour after hour of impenetrably rocky coasts had led him virtually to despair. Dehydrated and famished, he was beginning to consider the suicidal option of turning back. Until, that was he realised the storm was rising behind him, and his only choice was to run before it and hope beyond hope that he'd spy somewhere to land before the tempest engulfed him. He was an inexperienced and fair-weather sailor and didn't fancy his chances amongst such large waves.

So he could hardly believe his good fortune when he spotted three sails heading for land, although quite where they were going he could not imagine. Nevertheless, his desperation led him to steer towards them and follow them into the narrow and hidden entrance beyond the oddly shaped rock.

Copying their actions, he too dropped his sails as he could see the flukey winds would dash him against the sharp rocks on either side of him. And then, when to his horror the tidal waters rushed in behind picked him up and forced him forwards, all he could do was battle with his tiller and crash pell mell through the labyrinthine passage. Fortunate beyond anything he could have wished for (and beyond the experiences of the Coldharbour folk), he was lifted by a fluke wave through the Curve. His keel screamed as the tips of the rocks tore the underside of his boat, but his luck held and the small craft was not completely breached. It turned out that the small boat only a fool would take out to sea was just shallow enough to pass the channel and survive.

And what a sight greeted him as he rounded the final corner and entered the crater!

Surrounded on all sides by colossal mountains, some still snow-capped even now in mid-summer, with, from the foot of the sheer mountains a beautiful pastoral scene. Short trees, animals feeding in meadows and even fields of grain - all at improbable angles which no one would choose if flatter options were on offer. Clearly space was at a premium and options were not in plentiful supply, with the housing squeezed in almost to the water's edge.

As Arlaf had observed, Aldred was unaware that if he'd simply steered for shore, the current from the dissipating Surge would have washed him to land. His instinct was to get himself to the village as quickly as he could - not least because there was a fair old leak caused by the passage through Curve. Equally unaware of the Elder's disparaging comments, he was rather pleased with his tacking skills as he worked his way to the shore.

As he got closer, he realised that virtually the whole village must be there to greet him. Which was a good thing, probably, as it almost certainly meant that visitors from the outside hardly ever came. Thus they would be unaware of the Imperial proclamations to capture and hand in the renegade Aldred. Definitely a good thing!

A less good thing was the amount of water now in the bottom of the boat, slowing his approach and making it increasingly likely that it would sink before he reached the shore. Not disastrous but embarrassing, somewhat undermining his plan to present himself as a mighty and impressive Mage. Having to swim the last few yards would undermine the image he planned to project.

Fortune, though, apparently, was remaining on his side as a sharp gust of wind blew up and propelled him to the waters edge just moments, he was sure, before the vessel would have sunk. With considerably less panache than Luke had managed an hour earlier, Aldred gratefully clambered over the side as hands hauled in his boat and secured it. Grim-faced villagers reached out and pulled him in, too, as he stumbled, saving him from an undignified fall just at the last minute. He smiled his thanks and thought to himself, "Could've been better, could've been worse."

His smile reflected the relief he felt that despite betraying the Emperors, he had succeeded in fleeing their armed forces, Mages and spies and could look forward to a period of respite in apparent sanctuary. Nevertheless he was also aware that this was where the hard part was about to begin.

3 DECISIONS AND JUDGEMENTS

Luke sat sulking. He'd done that a lot recently. He knew it didn't look good to do so and he was painfully aware that his image as blessed with Feeling, a prodigious provider of much-needed fish and, in the minds of some a potential clan chief one day, had taken a hell of a battering already. Leading an Outlander into the secret sanctum of Coldharbour was bad enough, but, to be honest, to sit around whining and sulking wasn't helping his image one iota. He knew that, but he just couldn't help himself. The ancient crie de coeur of the teenager over the centuries; "It wasn't my fault ... it's just not fair!" just kept playing constantly through his brain. And the only physiological / psychological response possible in a young man, it seemed was a deep sulk.

Additionally, he was painfully aware that his initial expectation of impressing Marsha had also been blown out of the water. This, together with the fact that Olaf and Jarnock seemed to be reintegrated into the village life almost without a blemish on their reputation, wound him up even more. Meanwhile, accusing eyes were cast on him everywhere he went. Which is why he chose not to go anywhere, but simply sit and sulk and await the verdict of the interminable Elders meeting.

How long did it take to decide a moderate and fitting punishment for leading three boats fishing against the Weather-guard's advice? How long to add to it for leading in an Outlander? A few weeks' grounding plus perhaps some menial tasks was what he expected and, to be honest, was what would be fair. The Outlander was safely in their hands and could cause no harm. If they thought him a threat, well they could ensure he never escaped, could they not? Entering without Feeling was pretty miraculous - but since he'd been following Luke, he'd had good fortune on his side. He'd need more than that to ever escape because, if entering without Feeling was hard, exiting without it was virtually impossible. Aldred was a scrawny, weak little man. He'd never overpower anyone, forcing them to sail him out, so he was forever quarantined in Coldharbour. Serve him right if they allocated all the crappy jobs to him, Luke reckoned. Olbe the dung-collector had died and left a vacancy recently. That'd do.

So why take so long to come to a decision? That's what caused Luke's deep sulks and left him perplexed and frustrated. How could it take a week of deliberations? When had an Elders' conclave met for such a long time ever before? Even meetings to elect a new Chief - famously long ones - were said to take only a couple of days! No one could remember a seven-day gathering with food brought to the Meeting House and the only activity seen when grim-faced Elders left to relieve themselves, each one refusing to meet anyone's eyes, least of all Luke's.

The Outlander had been in there since day three, and never once had Luke been invited to give his side. How could they come to any sort of a conclusion - any fair sort anyway - when they didn't listen to him? The guy whose fresh fish was being daily shipped in to feed the Elders, while they considered so frustratingly slowly?

Too many questions. Too much to wonder. So much to cause him to sulk.

And so he sulked.

Finally, on the ninth day, Luke was summoned to join the conclave; not to be heard, but to be told their decision, ground out in the face, they said, of an unprecedented situation. A threat, they'd agreed, was to the very existence of the hidden village. And if Luke had cause to sulk before, his sense of injustice was multiplied ten-fold when told what their the verdict was!

"A year? A whole blasted year? The youth with the most Feeling in generations? The most productive fisher in the village? And you want to ground me for a year? And give me Olbe's job? Call yourself Elders? Call yourselves wise? What harm have I done that justifies ...?"

But Luke's tirade was cut short by the Chief. "Hold your tongue, traitor! Say one more word and it will be two years. After what we have discussed, you are fortunate you have a chance to redeem yourself."

"But," Luke tried once again, weakly, though, for he never got further than one word, as he caught the saddened look in his father's eyes.

"No buts, boy!" said Chief Alford, "And listen to the rest of your punishment."

Defeated, the youth dropped his head in horror at the thought that there could be more and worse to come.

"In that year you will not only be restricted to Coldharbour, not only be occupied as Dung Man, you will have the special role of being the link between the Outlander Aldred and the village. Your role will be to educate him in the ways of our community. He will be your constant companion and fellow Dung Man, and only if you succeed in our view as an Eldership will you ever ... and I mean ever ... be allowed to fish, let alone to use your prodigious Feeling powers again. We will test you by testing him. Now go and learn the skills of the Dung Man. No buts. Go!"

And he went.

4 DUNG MEN

Luke learnt the role of the Dung Man pretty quickly, which wasn't surprising since it was a fairly easy job, traditionally reserved for the least able of the village folk - Simples like Olbe. One of the many downsides of a relatively small enclosed population, without the opportunity to intermarry with outsiders, was the high rate of Simples. The positive was that within the benevolent society in Coldharbour all folk, no matter how able (or disabled) could be found a role to contribute. However, the Simples were less resistant to disease, and the outbreak of flu the previous winter had decimated their numbers, including the last incumbent of the job.

Nevertheless, Luke took it up with surprising alacrity. His rage at his punishment was such that it had rapidly cured his sulks and transformed them into an inferno, a high level of energy that he invested in his new work role.

And Aldred was a ready assistant, even if Luke steadfastly refused to communicate with him in any way other than grunts and finger pointing. But the essence of the task was essentially simple: collecting everybody's fire ash and human waste around the village daily and transporting it to the edges of the fields, where a number of the surviving Simples mixed it with inedible fish remnants and animal manure to make a passable fertiliser. It was a job that hardly needed much verbal communication.

However, Luke knew that in due course he would be forced to start talking, since the Elders would eventually insist he either fulfil his role as Outlander educator or be stuck as Dung Man forever. But when 'in due course' should become 'now' remained in the balance for some weeks.

It was loneliness in the end that opened the door to the breakthrough. Snubbing his friends, who had tried initially to sympathise, had simply driven them first to distance themselves from him and eventually to disdain. Luke's high levels of Feeling had led to a certain arrogance. It also dawned on him that perhaps his friends had hung out with him as a natural mover and shaker, and not because they actually liked him.

Now that in his rage he had alienated them, they basically ignored him or, worse still, sniggered as he pushed his dung barrow along the village passages. Luke found himself more alone than he'd ever been and the only option turned out to be to communicate with Aldred before the Elders forced him to do so. Loneliness, plus a week following a nasty bout of diarrhoea and fever caused by Luke failing to wash his hands properly after work. Healthcare was limited in Coldharbour and Luke became so sick eventually that the Healer had shrugged and suggested he could do no more him. Aldred, however, had continued to care for him, sought herbs on the upper slopes to treat him with, meanwhile continuing the tasks of village Dung Man.

In Luke's weakened condition, his rage faltered. Once he'd recovered his strength and returned to work, he discovered the grace to thank Aldred. He also saw in Aldred's humble response, the possibility of friendship. Thus, as Luke took up his job once again collecting the waste, he also began his role as Outlander teacher.

"So what do you want to know about Coldharbour?' he asked as they skirted the Meeting House.

"Everything would be best!" replied Aldred wryly, "But it would be good to start with history. I mean how long has this settlement been in existence? Why have I never heard of this place? How have you managed to keep yourselves secret so long?"

"How long we've been here is never told. Indeed, it's often occurred to me that our storytellers try very hard to avoid even suggesting how many generations we have been here. All I know is that our ancestors were fleeing from something very bad - so bad that that they decided we should never know exactly what it was."

"Haven't you ever wondered what that might be?" asked Aldred, incredulously.

"I have, but you have to understand the whole ethos of our founding is that it was so bad we are meant to understand we are better off not knowing what we fled from? I suspect that the concept of 'something really, really bad' is supposed to make us too fearful of the outside world to explore further than the seas near the entrance to Coldharbour."

Aldred thought about this for a while as they reached the outhouse of one of the settlement's larger houses. As usual, it took extra effort to lift and hold open the particularly heavy flap so that Luke could remove the family's offerings. As they wheeled the barrow away, he asked, "But you've wondered?"

Luke hesitated. He understood his role as being to introduce the outsider (indoctrinate him even) to the ways of Coldharbour - to get him to feel that this was a good place to live, a good place to settle and reduce his inclination to escape. What Aldred had not been told, but Luke assumed would be the case, was that if the Elders decided Aldred would not settle and be a positive influence, he would be Silenced. The benevolence of Coldharbour was limited by its obsessions with secrecy and survival.

Yet, obtusely, this first conversation was already kindling within himself a deeply-held curiosity about what his forebears had feared? Just as Aldred needed to learn what life was like here in the enclave, so the Elders had inadvertently offered Luke an equal opportunity to answer his own questions. It was a key moment in Luke's life. Did he play the Elders' game, or did he feed his own appetites?

Luke opted for the latter and replied, tentatively, "Yes ... I suppose so. But I'm supposed to be telling you about here - not wondering about 'out there'."

"I might be able to help, you know. We might be able to do both?"

Luke was saved from making a reply as they reached another outhouse and made a routine collection. In fact it took him some minutes before he finally said, "So what are you suggesting?"

"Well, how about this? I'm guessing you're interested in the world outside. I come from there and know what is going on out there. I also think that somehow the history out there has led to the life you have in here. I need to know what life is like here - and you've been charged with telling me that so I can settle. But that is hardly fair, since the information transfer is only one-way. So, how would you feel if we made an exchange? As you tell me about life here, I tell you about the outside?"

It took quite a while before Luke told Aldred that he agreed to the arrangement. A surprising length of time, since his heart leapt at the very prospect of hearing more of the wider world. Whereas deep suspicion and fear of life beyond Coldharbour was instilled into the villagers almost from weaning, Luke had always wondered what lay beyond the horizon he saw while he was out fishing.

All fishermen were trained to flee for the haven of home at even the hint of a sail on the horizon (a rare enough event, as it happened), but Luke had always turned with a slight reluctance and the half hope that his sail would tear and he might inadvertently be caught up by the Outlander ships. Despite this, he couldn't fight his initial, almost visceral revulsion at being close to a real life Outlander - a feeling which at first seemed to cause almost more nausea than the human excrement that he was forced by his new circumstances to deal with on a daily basis.

And since they had now moved into a more closely-packed section of the village - with an abundance of outhouses to service - he had the opportunity to seem too busy to respond to the enticing suggestion. Eventually, however, their barrows were filled and the walk to the fields offered them the opportunity for conversation again.

"Have you thought long enough about my suggestion?" Aldred asked.

"Probably, and I confess I'm tempted. However, I'm not sure I should and I'm not sure I trust you to tell me the truth anyway. How would I know you weren't making it all up - and making fun of me in the process?"

"Ah trust ..." smiled Aldred. "An interesting concept. I innocently sail behind other boats to flee the threat of a storm, and am told I must stay in what I thought was a short-term haven for a lifetime. And you don't think I have trust issues too? So what if what I tell you is a whole pack of lies? They might be interesting lies that could brighten up your dreary dung-filled days! And besides, has it not occurred to you that the Elders might have meant you to inadvertently find out what you can about me? How dangerous I am? How I might seek to pump you for the way to escape your village's clutches and avoid an eternity of dung-collecting?"

"Oh I can tell you how to escape, if you're interested," snapped back Luke. "Feeling."

"Feeling?" replied a perplexed Aldred. "I've heard mention of feeling but it doesn't make any sense. Feeling what, for goodness sake? Anyone I ask says it's your job to tell, and then they just clam up."

"Feeling is something that some of us have and some don't. And those who do have it can have different levels of Feeling ability. I for instance am said to have the highest levels in anyone born in recent years. Other young people have Feeling, but some can barely sense the tide at all. That's why it's so wrong to stop me sailing and reduce me to shovelling crap like Simples and ..."

"I'm sorry? I simply don't understand what you're talking about, Luke. What have feelings and tides got to do with each other?"

"Not 'feelings' it's 'Feeling' - the ability to sense the water below, recognise the rising and falling and most importantly the coming of the Surge."

"The Surge?" asked and increasingly confused Aldred.

So Luke explained the nature of the winding and shallow entrance to the volcanic bowl that served as the harbour of the village. How the sailer could use Feeling to sense the rising and falling of the tides to time entry and exit without de-hulling their boats. Further, the gift of Feeling meant he could sense where the fish were below his boat, and know precisely where to cast his nets. It transformed his fishing abilities.

He concluded, "You might think you could steal one of our boats and readily escape, but without Feeling you would never reach the open sea! Your entry was very, very fortunate, and only possible because you followed and mimicked our actions in front. If I had opened my eyes and spotted you by looking backwards, I could've readily scuppered you by changing my route, and timing it so your mirrored actions would've led you to disaster."

Aldred was incredulous. "You sailed through there with your eyes shut?"

"Mostly, though with my levels of Feeling, I am capable of looking around a bit too. But yes, Feeling is generally better used without distraction. Most of my friends simply can't manage without complete concentration."

Aldred stopped walking for a moment, and then, nodding and smiling he re-started up the now sloping path. "I see. And it makes sense suddenly. I knew I could sense something in you. It's just it's different in you, and I dismissed it. However, now you've explained it I think I understand."

"Nobody understands Feeling. We just have it and use it. You can't explain it," said Luke dismissively.

"Oh I can. I surely can. I know magery when I see it and what you've just told me is clearly exactly that, and …"

But before Aldred could utter another word Luke had punched him harder than he had ever been hit before. He collapsed in shocked silence, clutching his chin and fearing a broken jaw.

"Don't you ever say any such thing and don't you ever talk to me again!" said Luke, clearly distraught and almost overwhelmed with anger.

"I won't. I won't!" Aldred reassured him, while spitting out a mouthful of blood, grateful there wasn't a tooth in it. "Don't worry, we'll talk of other things."

But inside, Aldred felt a deep and overwhelming relief as three things gelled within him.

First, was a certainty that he knew magery when he encountered it: no matter how strange and abnormal it was: no matter how strongly it was denied. Second was the surety that he now knew how he was going to escape from Coldharbour. It was going to take some time and an inordinate amount of tact, guile and patience - but escape he would. And third, he was confident that they would indeed talk of Mages and that it would be this conversation which would open the door to this escape.

5 HISTORY (AND THEIR STORY)

It was some days until the pair talked again - but not as long as Aldred had prepared himself for. In the same way that loneliness initiated the first conversation, over time it was simply boredom that did the trick eventually. That, and a jammed dung trapdoor that for some reason simply would not budge. "I suppose you could try some of your famous magery?" joked Luke before crashing his barrow into the trap in frustration. When to his surprise this actually unjammed it, Aldred roared with laughter and suggested Luke's own magery seemed to have done the trick!

Laughter is a miraculous healer and the hours of silence seemed to disappear, initially in short exchanges but later in full-blown conversations. Plus an apology. "Never any harm in an apology," thought Aldred, plus a tacit agreement not to again mention Mages for the time being.

However, as time passed and spring moved into summer, the exchange of information took on more meaning. As Luke told tales of the seasons and the way Coldharbour had developed, Aldred gained a deeper understanding of the number of generations it must've been in existence. Eventually he was able to share his insight.

"Luke, I know it is supposed to be you telling me the history of your home. However, I think I have worked out how your people came to be here."

It was lunchtime. Months of working together had led to a pattern of working harder in the mornings to be free an hour after noon for a relaxed lunch by Central, the stream that led from the high mountains down to the crater. Central was wider and faster than the other brooks running towards the village and was used more for washing and cleaning than drinking water - so they would not get in trouble for swimming there and potentially contaminating it with the results of their labours. They had washed and were ready to eat when Aldred made his statement and Luke was as open as he was ever likely to be to the implicit offer.

"How can you know my history when I have shown over and over how little I know about it?" he asked.

"I've been thinking about the time it must have taken to develop to the stage you are. The age and the style of your buildings gave me another clue."

"Ok tell me! I'm all agog."

"There is a problem. In order to tell you, I need to mention something, and last time I mentioned it you nearly broke my jaw. I know we've joked about it since but, well I don't know. It's just that I value the ability to eat …!"

"You can mention Mages and magery - just don't bloody dare suggest I'm tainted with it. We have nothing to do with such awful things here, and I …"

"No worries, Luke. Let me tell you the story, and then we can talk about 'awful things' in due course. Deal?"

"Deal."

And so Aldred told the story - beginning with the Great Age. It was said that during the Great Age, people didn't depend upon animals to travel, using mechanical things known as 'mersheens,' which it's said were run by somethings called 'syence' and 'teck'.

Strange but entrancing words, which left Luke gasping for more.

Some even claimed that in the Great Age there were mersheens that flew in the air, though many thought that fanciful, and there was little evidence of such things. Humans had spread all over the globe and could communicate across vast distances. Their abilities were great. However, there was a dark side to the period. Their lust for power undermined their undoubted successes. Conflict and war were as common as the fruits of their tecks.

Not only that, the effects of their use of energy changed the climate detrimentally, resulting in sudden and irreversible rising of the sea levels. Wide scale flooding led to land wars breaking out and the inevitable result was a terrible conflagration in a disastrous catastrophic war, in which they unleashed their most destructive and fatal weapons.

This was followed by a long period known as The Forgetting when some of those who survived tried to hold onto the abilities of the past, whilst others, treating such tecks as the cause of their troubles, sought instead to suppress knowledge and to persecute those interested in syence

It took a long time to tell the story and it filled many lunchtime breaks. Words such as teck, mersheen, gineering and syence were so far beyond Luke's experience that it was evident how overwhelmingly the Forgetters had gained their victory. And having seen in his travels the devastated plains still showing evidence of great conflicts past, there was a part of Aldred that could not deny that syence and evil came from the same stable, even if his own knowledge of such things was limited at best.

"And so, many generations after The Great Age, a century or so after The Forgetting, the land was essentially settled into three Kingdoms. To the north lay Ruark - the mountainous lands with its wild people who lived nomadically in the rough terrain. Holding a fierce independence and loyalty to their king, they occasionally raided the lowlands of Southfleet - but generally they were pretty self-sufficient and learnt over time to trade their wild produce for the more domesticated animals and crops of the southerners.

"Here was the largest kingdom stretching across the central prairies, where folk concentrated upon crop growing and animal farming. Rich in food and people, it could keep at bay raids from the mountain folk but could never mount enough energy to win a war beyond their flatland comfort zones. Nor could they impose their will upon the westerly folk who lived in the sea kingdom of The Islands - multiple isles lying off the mainland. Nominally this third locale was a single realm, but in reality the Islands were more a loosely-held confederacy, whose clans and villages elected a king and stuck together on the basis that they needed someone to negotiate trade with Southfleet and to bring them together when a land-based King suddenly got it into his head that he could run things in the offshore realm."

"And did that happen often?" asked Luke.

"More rarely over time - the period was pretty stable, from what I can gather. Until the Mages came."

"Where did they come from - if all the people left were those in the three Kingdoms?'

"That is a mystery - but I think they essentially came from the eastern edges of Southfleet - beside the ravaged lands. Something in the area, left over from the conflagrations, had led to changes in people. Some were horrible alterations to their bodies - longer limbs, grotesque body forms - and many were fatal. If detected, such affected folk were often ostracised or even killed, I am afraid.

"But some, we think, developed special abilities that were not obvious and they were able to keep these secret."

Luke was increasingly confused. "What sort of abilities?"

"Mostly ones using the mind? People arose who could talk over great distances, or move objects without lifting them, or control the bodies of others. Initially people called it witchcraft and those found with abilities were often killed. But some of them stuck together and, using their powers in combination, gradually led others to safety. Especially if they could get themselves close to a king, which is what happened over time. The kings became surrounded by a cortege of 'protectors' who gradually took control of the court. Working together - and with the ability to communicate with each other they effectively merged the three Kingdoms into one in a bloodless coup - well a battle-less one, anyway. It was pretty brutal nevertheless, from what I can gather.

"The Mages began to run what became known as the Empire and after a while the strongest of the Mages became the Emperor, with his cohorts sent in groups throughout the realm as Governors, and law enforced by troops of the Imperial Corps. This all eventually settled down to a new normality for a generation or two."

"So the Mage Emperor founded a dynasty of his successors?"

"Ah no. I failed to mention that the nature of being a Mage often meant that they were unlikely to father children - something in the nature of magery seemed to make fertility a problem. The most powerful Mages rarely, if ever, produced an heir. Even if they did, their children were never as gifted as their sires."

"So how did they continue their line?" wondered Luke.

"Basically they didn't, I suppose. Somehow they had an in-built loyalty to other Mages in the early generations, and saw it as a matter of self-interest to maintain the status quo of Mages in power. Previous periods of persecution had led them to stick together and cooperate. They knew they were like a race apart, hated and, more to the point, feared, by the general populace. It was in the interests of even the weaker Mages that other Mages ran the Empire. And it has to be said that even those who despised their ways agreed that the Mages ran a jolly efficient regime."

Luke interrupted again. "So how did they continue their dominance if they weren't themselves breeding more Mages?"

"They used Seekers to find those with magery within them - and before you ask me what a Seeker is, perhaps it would help if I told you the different types of magery? Generally the greatest Mages were the Melders - those with the power to control the minds of other people."

"People? More than one at a time?"

"Oh yes indeed. Sure, some could manage only a handful at a time - but the Great Mages - the ones who usually made it to be Emperor - could control a roomful. Half a dozen powerful Melders could hold back a crowd. They could even hold sway over other Mages if necessary.

"The second most influential were the Porters - those who could use their powers to move or deflect things with the power of thought. Throw a spear at a Porter and it would never reach its target."

"What if it were thrown from behind?" asked Luke.

"They seemed by and large to have such an awareness of the physical world around them that they could generally sense anything approaching them. And again Porters could work together and combine their powers so the sum was greater that way. It is said that in the great battles that resulted in the subsuming of the Islands that ships containing half a dozen Porters sailed between massed fleets of Islander boats, lifting them out of the waters, ripping out a number of planks and then dropping them back into the water to flounder and sink."

"Lifted a whole boat? Really?'

"No not a boat - a ship, big enough to hold twenty or so people. I'm telling you, these Porters are mighty powerful - especially in groups. But they could rarely challenge the Melders unless they had a bit of melding ability as well. Plus a group of Porter friends to support their bid for the throne."

"Some had more than one power?"

"Sometimes - with one dominant - but yes. Often too they had a touch of the third power - that of the Pather. The greatest of these could actually read minds - read the very thoughts of those around them. Some could even project thoughts into the minds of people - though that was pretty rare. But most had more of an ability to sense moods, and intentions - and of course, tell whether people were telling the truth. Clearly this gift is helpful and most powerful Mages found it incredibly useful to have a Pather as an ally, but the ability was never a match for the other two types of Mage.

"Finally, a lesser ability lay with the Seekers, those who could innately sense the power of magery in others."

"That doesn't sound that useful to me," suggested Luke.

"True. Hence I call it a lesser ability. However, in an environment where those Mages in power need successors outside their families, someone was needed to identify the Mages of the future. So the Seekers wandered the Empire, sensing among the young of the populace at large and finding the Mages of the future."

"They didn't take them away as children from their parents, did they?"

"Oh yes indeed. Mind you, once the parents realised their child was 'afflicted' as they would see it, the child's life was in danger anyway. The knack of a Seeker would be to identify a gift before its tell-tale signs were evident. You will remember your violent reaction to my suggestion of magery within you? Just consider what it would have been if you thought your child had it! Especially in a society where Mages are perceived as the evil oppressors."

"I suppose I see what you mean. So the Seekers took the children away to be brought up and assessed for their abilities?"

"Indeed - though a good Seeker could essentially tell the areas where a Mage would be gifted."

"And were Mages always male?"

"In the early years, yes, but later generations revealed a number of female Mages - some even with prodigious powers. And in some ways therein lay the seeds of the Mage Wars because male power politics were essentially simple, based on strength, power, ability. There was a complicated system of selection of who would be Emperor - games of skill and tests of abilities. Many of the succession battles were brutish and sometimes fatal - but once an Emperor was selected, all the rest happily swore loyalty to him, and until his powers began to fail nobody ever challenged him again. Mind you, most failing Emperors realised that it was in their interest to step down graciously and allow a more effective Mage to take up the reins, and continue to be protected by their peers. Not only that, it was possible in a violent battle for Mages to burn themselves out in a conflict and end up powerless, empty of magery and suddenly very vulnerable. They might have been simplistic and ambitious - but generations of Mages recognised their common bond of self-interest! Mages will always be in the minority, and it ill-behoved such a group to be constantly looking inwards - the real enemy was always the ungifted outside the circles of magery.

Some of the female Mages were somehow cleverer, less brutish and, since they were far more often fertile, often much more ambitious for their children than the men had ever had a chance to be. Factions developed, conflicts erupted and resulted eventually in the Mage Wars.

"It was a horrible time, with civilians forced into battle by Porters and Melders completely against their wills. It was a war of no interest to them but, as always in a nation controlled by Mages, the innocent, ungifted folk became dragged in and suffered immensely."

"How long ago was this?"

"A couple of hundred years ago, on and off. During that time some among the ungifted populace developed a cult of purity, very much rooted in the old concept of the Forgetters. Wishing to purge themselves of magery and all the violence resulting from it, they aimed to escape. They fled to the Islands and to the mountainous areas to the north of old Ruark."

"To set up new communities without magery?"

"Yes indeed. But also passionately believing in wiping all memory of history. They foolishly believed that if they knew nothing of where they came from that they would somehow never make the mistakes of the past. Stories of where they came from were proscribed and children brought up ignorant of their roots and passionately indoctrinated against anything to do with magery. Strangers were treated as highly suspicious, labelled as Outlanders and if encountered, usually killed."

"That sounds a great deal like us here in Coldharbour."

Aldred laughed. "I did say I'd tell you where your people came, from didn't I? The whole ethos of your village reeks of 'Forgetter' - not to mention that the style of buildings is so similar to that period."

Luke was aghast. "You mean to say that we are a Forgetter colony? We were founded by people fleeing the Mage Wars? Really? That's fascinating."

"What's more fascinating is that you are fascinated by your past, Luke. The natural instinct of a Forgetter colony member is to be horrified at the mere thought of the past. I had a feeling however that you were different. That you might be the exception, being open to questions and uncertainty."

"And story too. I've always wanted to hear stories and know about Outland. Our stories are really dull!"

"But fortunately you had enough sense not to ask too many questions of your Elders."

"Why fortunately?"

"In most Forgetter colonies those who show too much interest in the past tend to end up shut up. Permanently!"

"Yeah, I can imagine that. I never really thought about it, but I sort of instinctively knew not to probe - even though I was dying to know. Desperate to hear the stories and to learn more."

"Well thank goodness you had that instinct I say. Execution in Forgetter communities tends to have a euphemistic name, like 'Dampen,' Excised' or ..."

"Or 'Silenced?'"

"Exactly! Is that what's it's called here?"

Luke nodded grimly as he realised the repercussions of what had just been said. After a while, though, his inquisitiveness won out. "We can talk about my community's history later - for now I just want to know how the Mage Wars concluded. How and when did they end?"

"About thirty seasons ago, with one mighty final battle. Generations of battles had resulted in the death of hundreds of the ungifted and scores of Mages met their end too. The victorious Emperor was Camrin, who was very firmly in control, jealously ensuring any other Mage with any significant power was well and truly out of the scene and unable to challenge his dominance."

"How did he do that?"

"By killing any Mage with any hint of great power - even in childhood."

"That's terrible! How could he kill children? And how could he tell who was a future threat?"

"Very easily - his wife, the Empress Magrat is a Seeker (as well as a hugely gifted Pather), who tests all children brought in and callously disposes of any she deems powerful enough to be a threat to them."

"But doesn't the Emperor need other Mages to maintain them in power?"

"Indeed they do - but none with the power to overthrow their hegemony. Vicious and vile they are, and cold and hard as nails. They argue it is in the interest of the Empire to avoid future Mage Wars - but in truth it is only in their own interest."

Luke sat in shocked silence for a while. The sheer enormity and horror of what he had just heard made him wonder if he might've been better off without his illicit interest in the Outlander world having been fed.

But that interest could not be dampened. Other questions kept popping up. "Who," he eventually asked "will they be succeeded by?"

"Good question. It turns out they are an exceptional couple in more ways than one. Powerful Mages they have given birth to a son who is in turn powerfully gifted. Their succession is assured at least for this generation. So they make sure that no Seeker-found Mage can threaten them or their son.

"A year ago a Seeker discovered a young woman whose powers had been missed before. They were amazing and unique but he feared that if the Emperor got wind of this girl's powers, he would simply kill her. And he couldn't bear it again. He'd seen too many go that way. She was a nice kid and he couldn't risk not declaring her and passing her by and risking discovery by a future Seeker."

"So what did he do?'

"He hid her. Explained to her the Mage-craft within her and the threat to her life, and then persuaded her to run away with him and hide her where the Mages could not reach her."

"That must've been a bit of a risk?"

"Oh yes. Very risky! And somehow Camrin got wind of it and came after that Seeker, swearing if he caught up with him for his betrayal it would be him as well as the girl who would bear the brunt of his wrath."

"So what did he do?"

"The only thing he could - flee. Flee as fast and as far as he could go."

"Terrifying. Terrible! … And how do you know about this?"

"Promise you won't hit me if I tell you?"

"OK - but why would I hit you?"

"Because the last time I suggested a Mage was one of us, you decked me! But I'm going to trust your word. I'm going to trust you … and tell you how I know this. And I know it to be true because I am that Seeker on the run."

"You a Mage?"

"A low-level Mage. A lowly Seeker. In the eyes of the Mage elite a rubbish Mage even - but yes, me a Mage. I'm sorry to say."

Luke looked at him for a moment, smiled and, as much to his own surprise as to Aldred's relief, burst out with, "Awesome! That is awesome!"

6 UNFOLDINGS

It took a while for Aldred's tale to sink into Luke's subconscious but his instincts for self-preservation were so automatic that it never once occurred to him to share anything of his news.

As if he had anyone to share with, so isolated was he, by association with an Outlander on the one front and by the taboo of his current occupation on the other! Nevertheless, it took a few days before the mixture of euphoria and intrigue settled into properly formed questions and a direction to his thoughts.

Aldred, meantime was patient. He knew he'd dropped an almighty bombshell, despite Luke's initial enthusiastic response. It would take Luke some time to assimilate the tale he'd shared and the risk he'd taken. He was, though, confident not only that it was worth taking, but that the time was right to take it. Luke was intelligent enough to take on board the implications of what he had learnt, and also very clearly sufficiently counter-cultural, despite his Forgetter heritage, to assimilate it and come to the conclusion Aldred most desired. He awaited their next opportunity to talk, with confidence.

He was, however surprised by the initial direction of the conversation, when it did arise, on another balmy summer day when they had completed their tasks early, and after a refreshing swim and lunch by the riverside.

"So," began Luke, I suppose since you know so much about Coldharbour you have already worked out its problems?"

"Apart from those inherent in all Forgetter settlements you mean?"

"Which are?"

"In essence, that not knowing where you came from plus not understanding exactly what it is you are fleeing from, leaves you ultimately at risk, since you don't know what you fear?"

"Is that usual? I mean, have you encountered many such groups?"

"Well quite a few," replied Aldred, "because for all their insularity they have generally been so much against those I am fleeing that several times in my travels, they have offered me a safe haven. The thing is, though, that for all their separation from the Empire, none of them were as completely shut off as you are here in Coldharbour."

"And that is exactly our problem."

"How so?"

"I'm, supposed to have been telling you how we run, and how wonderful it all is, and on the face of it life here is pretty idyllic. We have a good climate, a safe environment and, overall, a reasonable place to live. We have a beneficent model of leadership that enables everyone, from the most to the least able to have a role and to contribute to the common good."

"Yes, it does seem remarkably stable and fair."

"It is. And though we understand the concept of 'rich' and 'poor' no such label applies here. Yes, some folk have bigger, better homes than others, and a degree of extra comfort, but the difference is marginal. And did you notice that when one of the Elders died recently, his widow and son moved to a smaller house?"

"Was that demanded?"

"No, not at all. Hoped for maybe, but not compulsory. She knew that there was a family with four boys, squashed into a much smaller place, and she volunteered to swap. It made sense for her and for them. But she didn't have to do it."

"Impressive. It's a level of selflessness that is rare in the Empire."

"Maybe, but it stems from one of two major problems we face. The first is our location. Safe and secure it may be from whatever we fear outside, nestled as we are between high mountains behind us and a virtually impregnable entrance. However, space is severely limited. We have grown larger over the years and frankly we are bursting at the seams, with nowhere else to expand to. If we build more houses it will be on agricultural land, further reducing our already limited ability to grow produce. Not to mention the shortage of wood. The trees we have we harvest in rotation, to ensure enough fuel, and we manage just about. But if we need wood for boat repairs or building, we have to sail around the coast to the mainland to gather timber. We have poor skills in tree-felling and our shallow boats can transport only limited amounts, plus there are the risks of discovery. We have badly needed a timber cull for over a year but the Elders have suffered one of their regular states of inertia. It's bad enough getting permission to sail out to fish. Unless old Garrick says the weather's perfect we can't even think about it - and without the fish to augment our diet, we are in danger of starvation in the long run. Having me hamstrung as Dung Man has made the Elders' job immensely easier, as they don't have to experience me constantly badgering them to let me out to fish!"

"I thought you were charged with telling me how wonderful it is here?"

laughed Aldred.

"I am - and in many ways it is indeed wonderful. But unless things change soon in some way, we are heading for disaster."

"Because of overcrowding? I've noticed quite a few empty houses on the outskirts of the settlement."

"That's cos of the flu we had last winter. It killed a number of us and reduced the pressures a bit, especially as it took mostly the older ones, plus quite a number of the Simples, who tend to be more vulnerable to infections, and who in turn offer us yet another challenge."

"I have to say that I think your offering of a valid role in your community for less able people is commendable. In the Empire they are often seen as a curse and rarely enabled to thrive. Few live to adulthood."

"That's as may be. But there seems to be something about being such a closed community that we are producing more and more Simples - a higher proportion every year. Plus a smaller and smaller number of us have Feeling. We don't just need wood and fish from outside, we actually need a fresh influx of people."

"And that is never going to happen with your Forgetter heritage."

"Exactly. Though it partly explains how you were able to persuade them to let you stay and not Silence you to save our anonymity. By the way, however did you do that?"

Aldred smiled wryly. "That was some challenge! But as I said before, I have met quite a few Forgetter villages and I guessed correctly you were one too. I think I know what rings their bells and ..."

"Sorry, but what is a bell?"

This time Aldred laughed. "Yes sorry, a turn of phrase! I realise that though much of our language is in common a village that wishes to keep its whereabouts secret wouldn't just not want to advertise its presence with bells, but wipe out the necessity of knowledge of bells, too. How do I explain? Well, a bell is a cast metal dome that when you hit it, resounds with a loud and musical noise. The noise is ringing - hence the analogy of ringing of bells. Does that help?"

"I suppose so. But it reminds me of another thing we're short of, which is metal, with is very limited. We re-use and recast, which in turn takes a lot of wood! We're short of all sorts of other materials too: we're heading towards a real crisis."

"I can see what you mean. Do the Elders realise this?"

"Not at all. They live in denial and stick rigidly to the founding principles of the colony: 'Hide from what's out there, don't ask what's out there and, what is more, make sure you hide!'"

"I have to say, I am amazed at a teenager like you realising all this all by yourself. Have you shared your concerns?"

"No, I wouldn't dare. You have no idea how closed their minds are. I had hoped that as I became more respected for what I as a fisher could offer, I might rise to the Eldership earlier than normal. My Father became an Elder relatively young, but sadly he wasn't minded to change things. The trouble was, the more impatient I was to fish, the less chance I had to be listened to. As you say, I am a mere teenager!"

"So do you have a solution?"

"Oh yes. But first I need to ask you a question."

"Certainly."

"You're a Seeker?"

"That's right."

"So how do you tell what sort of magery a person has?"

"That's even harder to describe than a bell! But I'll try. When I am near a person with a gift of magery I can sense something within them. A sort of aura that emanates from them. And the auras have differences that are, I suppose, a bit like flavours or textures? You know how you can distinguish between the different fish you catch? Well it's rather like that."

"And you can sense that difference? You can tell if someone is a Melder or a Pather just by their aura?"

"Yes. A bit like you sense the water and the tides below you, I suppose."

Luke looked uncomfortable for a moment and then asked the question that had been sitting unsaid for the whole conversation. "So that was why you suggested that Feeling is like a gift of magery?"

"I can't answer that."

"You can't answer that without saying that Feeling is a gift of magery you mean?"

Aldred looked at the ground for a bit and eventually said, "I told you, I value my ability to eat. My jaw can't take another slug last the last one and ..."

But Luke had no interest in fighting now. He was intrigued. The history of the land had opened his mind to possibilities and opportunities. Nothing would stop him pushing. "So which type of magery do you think Feeling is a part of? I mean I can't read minds, move objects or make people do things and ..."

"It's a different gift altogether. A new one I've not encountered before. I felt it when I followed you through the Curve. It's so difficult to describe, but, I suppose it's present and just there? Lying on you, like any of the various gifts do on other Mages I have encountered? And lying there on you all the time. It is odd and fresh and unusual, but you're right, it has the taste of magery - just a different flavour."

"So that's all there is to it? It's just an ability like others have, just different? How disappointing!"

"One minute you're horrified when I call you a Mage - and the next you're disappointed at the sort of Mage you are!"

"It's complicated!"

"Well at least you haven't thumped me this time, so I will take a risk and tell you more. Which is, as I think I said earlier, that sometimes people have more than one gift of magery?"

"Yes. What are you trying to tell me?"

"Well, Luke, the truth is I don't really know how to say this. Not exactly. Because you see, as well as the unfamiliar 'Feeling' flavour I can taste on you, there's something else. Something more. Another flavour, another magery texture to you that is also different, exotic, new."

Luke's face went pale with a strange mixture of horror and delight. "And what is it? What can I do? What gift have I got?"

"I'm sorry to say I have absolutely no bloody idea! You are double-blessed with new magery. Two new gifts. One Feeling and the other ... the other, powerful and intoxicating but ... I just don't know."

Luke stood up, infuriated, fists clenched tightly at his side. "That's nonsense. You're just saying it because you've never encountered Feeling before."

"No please, calm down. This is important - to you and to me, and indeed to Coldharbour. Feeling has a very distinct flavour and I can tell you all the others with it - Jenkers, Harold, Olaf, Bolser, Jarnock, half a dozen others including Garrick, whose weather-sensitivity is just another manifestation of the ability. Oh yes and Marsha and Aloric, and to a lesser extent, several other females."

"No not Marsha and Aloric - yes you're right about the others, but not them. Women don't have Feeling."

"You're right about your benevolent society here but I have to say you have a blindspot to women. You're hugely male-dominated and your attitudes have blinded you to the fact that women as well as men can be gifted. I mean how do you test if anyone has Feeling?"

"Take them on a boat through the Curve during a Surge and test their sensitivity."

"And have you ever taken a female there?"

"Of course not - women don't have Feeling they're ..."

"They've never been given the chance?"

"I suppose that's possible."

"Luke, that answer tells me exactly what I knew all along."

"Which is?"

"That you are different in more ways than having two gifts I've not met before. That you have an open mind almost unheard of in a Forgetter community. That there is hope for you and for me."

"And for Coldharbour too?"

"Oh yes. Very definitely. But for that to be realised, you and I need to do something together."

"And that is?"

"Can't you guess? I think you know."

"Yeah, I think you're right. We need to leave Coldharbour. We need to get out of here and bring some new blood into the community. Not to mention, find out what sort of Mage I am."

"You have no idea how relieved I am to hear you say that."

"Only cos I didn't hit you when you did!"

And though they collapsed with laughter, the enormity of what he had just said was already sinking in to Luke's subconscious!

7 ESCAPE FROM COLDHARBOUR

The next few days were enormously busy. The first harvest was approaching and the Dung Men were roped into the preparations, as it was traditional for most of the villagers to work together to bring in the crops. Even the elite, could sometimes join in so there was no way the lowly sewage collectors could be excused. But though opportunities for long conversations and lazy afternoons were gone, there was plenty of time for thinking and planning.

Nevertheless, Luke was finding it hard to work out a foolproof plan for their escape. The downside to the relatively little tidal movement within the crater was that there were houses almost down to the water's edge and, what is more, they almost all looked out over the lake. The chances of taking a boat and sailing out unnoticed were virtually nil, day or night. A long-lasting diversion or some other subterfuge would be needed to let them be the only boat to exit on an Outsurge. A foolproof plan was needed, and Luke was struggling to formulate one. Perhaps, now the current harvest period was coming to an end, they would get the chance to work on it?

However, events were taken out of Luke and Aldred's hands when someone else took over and implemented probably the only possible perfect escape plan - and one the two could never have dreamed of.

Believing that they had been careful in their choice of venue for their discussions, it had never occurred to them that they had been overheard, or that some element of their conversations had been reported to the Elders. Their arrest, then, was as unexpected as it was apparently disastrous.

One minute they were looking forward to a wash and a sleep after a morning of dung collecting, followed by a long, hot afternoon in the fields. The next they were being manhandled into the Meeting House, to be greeted by an already assembled Eldership. Luke had noticed their absence from the fields earlier, but had assumed that they had taken the chance of meeting to get out of the work.

Not so. It appeared they had been meeting to discuss news obtained from a spy who had reported a limited but damning portion of their most recent conversation. Aldred was charged with magery, Luke with consorting with and protecting a Mage - crimes he didn't even know existed!

Barely given a chance to defend himself, he ought to have played dumb and pretended it was the mischievous malice of whoever had pretended to overhear their conversations. That was what the older and wiser Aldred tried to do. But Luke's passion and his prior sense of grievance about the last few months betrayed him, as he inadvertently gave away again and again that what had been reported was in fact entirely accurate. The clincher was when Luke discovered that it was Marsha, the girl he had once had romantic plans for, who was the source of the information. His outrage at such treachery was yet deeper than if it had been one of his best friends and led to him betraying himself even more.

The Elders' decision was as inevitable as it was unanimous. Even Luke's father, Arlaf, had voted for them them to be Silenced in the only way the Coldharbour community used. The pair were taken away, tied up and held in the only house that held a lock and kept there without food or drink until a fisher could be spared to sail them out to sea and drop them overboard. There, bound and weakened by starvation, their end would be mercifully quick - or so it was deemed. Beneficent in general as a society, Coldharbour was indeed a classic Forgetter community whose instincts to close ranks and unify against the threats of the outside world were absolute, even if it meant disposing of a perceived weak link in their protective portfolio. Even if that meant execution.

Luke's father made no attempt to visit him to say goodbye, adding to several days of abject misery before his levels of consciousness began to fade as dehydration began to take effect.

It was almost a relief to find himself and Aldred bundled up and dragged one by one to the nearest boat just outside the Lock House. His vague thoughts included a degree of surprise that they were doing it in the middle of the day, for he had expected to have been taken out at night so that no-one would see the departure and upset sensibilities. Though there was a certain logic to carrying out the process while the whole village was in the upper fields, there was the additional level of irritation that they might've spared more than one person, so he wouldn't have needed to be literally dragged up a plank and rolled into the boat, landing in a painful and undignified manner on top of Aldred. But frankly he was beyond caring. His plans, his hopes and everything he had ever wished for were about to be washed away and silenced forever

He was, therefore somewhat surprised as the boat approached the exit to find his skipper reach down and hold a flagon of water to his lips.

Surprised or not, he gulped gratefully - even though a part of his mind reminded him he would be better off less, not more conscious. Aldred was similarly given water, then Luke's blindfold was removed and he was gently moved around to be made more comfortable.

As the water began to hit his system he was able to look around a bit. The skipper was at the helm but he could only see legs from where he lay. He could see considerable supplies of food, which was extremely strange as fishers rarely went outside for more than 24 hours, and a Silencing trip would mean a return at the next high tide six hours or so hence. He was also somewhat perturbed that the sailer seemed rather clumsy and inexperienced, and found himself rather arrogantly despising the amateurish technique he observed. The sails were taken down hugely untidily, and the keel didn't appear to be completely raised.

"They couldn't even give me a decent sailer to silence me," he thought glumly. "At this rate the silly bugger'll drown himself at the same time."

He shut his eyes again and began to Feel the deep counter Surge that was the driver for exiting from the Coldharbour crater. Somehow at a particular point of low tide, something valve-like within the curves caused an Outsurge, that was if anything more violent and unpredictable than the Surge that facilitated entry. This was a big one and it was coming … and any second now.

And when it did, it lifted and threw the boat forwards, rushing through the narrow curves beyond the Spires. Against his better judgement, Luke couldn't help but thrill to the Feeling of water, wood and Outsurge, and find himself admitting that the skipper was handling the boat safely and skilfully through what was a remarkably violent and technically difficult manoeuvre. "Left, right now, yes hard over right and then back again. Brilliant, just as I would have done." he thought to himself before Feeling the deep and almost sexual rush as they passed the Cleft Rock and shot into the open sea. Then keel down, sails up and back to traditional sailing - sailing on to his death. Ah well, he thought, at least he'd felt the Feeling and joy of one last passage.

But then more surprises.

More water was offered to drink and his ropes were untied. He was still helplessly weak, but no sensible executioner would release their prisoner so. Desperation might at any time give a condemned person the extra energy to overcome them! The only thing stopping Luke from launching an immediate assault was a consideration of when would be the best opportunity. And anyway there was time, as Aldred too was untied.

As Aldred was untied as well? Untying both of them was sheer craziness. He wondered what other surprises might await around the corner, as he steeled himself to attack. Then he hesitated as the fisher turned back around and he saw her face. The biggest surprise of the lot!

"Marsha? Marsha! What the hell are you doing here?" he asked through dried, cracked lips.

"Never mind that now. Explanations later," she replied, with a slight hint of panic. "We're out in the open sea, all Coldharbour saw us from the fields as we escaped and we need to get as much distance between us and them before the next Outsurge. I'm no sailor and you are. Let's get moving quickly and we'll talk later. If you want to live, for goodness sake, show me how to get these sails up, then get on the tiller and tell me what else to do!".

Part 2 - Outland

8 FREE!

Luke was cold and miserable, and the fire was taking far too long to dry him out. He was tempted, despite Aldred's orders, to add more wood it. He'd gathered plenty and there had been no-one in the locality. Why was Aldred being so blasted careful? And why did Marsha have to keep agreeing with Aldred all the time? Who was it who had sailed the boat for three days, including one of storm and rain (something he didn't admit he'd never done before)? Who was it who'd found three perfectly safe places to land, before Aldred finally agreed to one of them? And who had skilfully taken them in past large rocks and shallows and then perfectly landed them on that gentle beach by the riverside? Only for Aldred to tip the boat over getting out, causing them to lose it, together with most of their remaining stores and, most uncomfortably of all, to leave them all soaked to the skin?

And still whatever Aldred said went! Aldred was an Outlander and a stranger to her, whereas she'd known Luke all her life. But what could you expect of a person who could betray a life-long friend to the Elders? He'd thought of her as his likely mate before, yet now he could hardly understand what he had ever seen in her!

Then again, in truth, the way her wet fringe hung over her eyebrows was strangely alluring. But that was the way of harpies and traitors - they used their charms to trap you and stab you in the back. A back that, like the rest of him, was wet and bloody miserable!

And where, incidentally, was all-seeing, all-knowing Aldred? Perhaps he'd abandoned them, now he was free? How could they have been so stupid as to let the dirty Outlander out of their sight? He considered sharing his doubts but the only person to share them with was Marsha, and what did she know? She just sat there staring into the fire and hugging her knees. Where the hell was Aldred anyway?

Of course, if he'd been listening to the sounds around him instead of all that noise in his head, Luke might have heard his approach.

"Not the best of lookouts are you two?" asked a grinning Aldred, as he sat suddenly between the two. Lukes's grunt was about to be followed by a curse when he saw what Aldred had placed before them. It was a decent sized four-legged animal, that Luke had never seen before. But whatever it was, it looked like it would provide plenty of meat for the three of them. Though Marsha had thought to bring supplies, she had brought nothing to fish with, and they had not been able to supplement their food with anything while they had been at sea.

"What is it?" he demanded.

"Deer, they are called. Quite a young one. I was very fortunate that it had got itself caught in a bush. It had nearly struggled free when I stumbled across it, and it's a good job Marsha brought a decent knife, as I don't think I could've broken its neck in my condition."

"Well, glad she got something right," Luke sneered!

"Oh shut up and let's get this thing butchered! I thought you were starving," she retorted, and took up the knife proffered by Aldred. "Do you think we might have a bit more fire now? We'll never cook much on that thing, I'm afraid."

"Yes, I reckon so," replied Aldred. "I've scouted round even further than Luke did earlier and I think we're pretty safe for tonight."

"About time too," sniped Luke. "I said so earlier and ..."

Marsha's patience finally gave way. "Oh for goodness sake stop whinging. I'm cold and wet too. We're all cold and wet, but being dry is no help if we're dead. Aldred is the only person who has ever lived here in Outland territory. He's survived before and we need his wisdom and experience to survive too. You're a damn good sailor and a damn good fisherman and, for all I know, a blooming good Dung Man too. But that's it. That's all you know, all you've ever done! And Aldred has done more. We need to listen to him. You need to listen to him if we are going to survive. Now, the first step to surviving is getting this deer cooked, so excuse me if I get started. You might help by building up the fire like you've wanted to for the last few hours."

Muttering "Traitor," under his breath, Luke had little option but to comply ...

***

Some time later, with a stomach fuller than it had been for what seemed like months, considerably warmer, with the excess deer meat neatly wrapped up in large leaves, ready to transport for onward journeys, and nearly dry through, Luke was feeling rather better.

Very much better in fact, but still in no mood to forgive or forget. He had, though, decided to keep his mouth shut, for now.

Aldred, however, was ready to catch up on events and, as the light began to fade, he started the ball rolling. "So, Marsha, brilliant escape plan. I'm impressed how you fooled everyone, including us. But before I get around to asking why you did it, or why you came too, however did you know about our conversations? About the magery and everything? What you reported could only have been eavesdropped, and I was very careful to check there was nobody around before we started talking confidential stuff."

"You did, I noticed: but once you'd checked you tended to relax and not notice if I crept in closer after a bit. You said we weren't good lookouts, but actually you're not that good yourself!"

"Ouch!" laughed Aldred, though Luke just grunted again. "So why were you there in the first place?" asked Aldred. As far as anyone knew we were just there for a wash and a swim."

Marsha looked a bit embarrassed as she smiled coyly and said, "Exactly!"

Luke's resolution not to engage in the conversation snapped immediately. "You what? You came to look at us bathing naked? That's disgusting! That's …"

" … exactly what you and your friends do every summer at the girls' spot on Central. And don't even try to deny it! We've all seen you, trying to be invisible by that large bush that's supposed to be providing us with cover! Why do you think you never got to see very much? Think we're all prim and proper? No. Just smart. Smarter than you realise, eh?"

"Obviously," laughed Aldred, though Luke still looked shocked. "And obviously as interested in boys as they are in you. Forgetter communities are no different in that respect! And did you come alone or with friends? I'm just wondering how many others may have seen my delectable body!"

"Don't flatter yourself, Aldred, I wasn't coming to see you. Not initially anyway. And on my own actually. Fortunately too, judging by what I heard too! One afternoon I happened to stumble past you both there splashing in the water and, intrigued, I snuck in and found a convenient hidey-hole to sit in. After I realised this was your regular haunt, I found it often coincided with my own free time so I took to regularly listening in. It was fascinating. Like Luke I have always wanted to know more about Outlands and stuff but had always feared asking.

"Then when you said I had Feeling too - and Luke denied it - I couldn't stop wanting to know more, because I finally understood why I didn't fit in properly at Coldharbour. When you started to talk of leaving I just knew that I wanted out too, and I started to think about a plan for escape like you did. All your plans were fatally flawed or far too complex to have a chance of working, but once harvest began, I realised that everyone would be in the fields, at the farthest point from the shoreline. I knew that we'd never get leave for all three of us be released from harvest duty at once. But then I happened to stroll past the Lock House, and the thought occurred to me that if you two were in there, and if it were me who was guarding you, and if it coincided with an Outsurge in the middle of the day ..."

"There's an awful lot of ifs and buts there," Luke almost spat out. "And in the meantime we went through the hell of judgement before the Elders, sentence to silencing and then nearly dying of dehydration and all!"

"Yes, I'm sorry about all that, but I'd worked out the timetable. I chose a good time to report you and I knew they'd pass sentence pretty quickly. It actually worked out pretty well to time. They took an extra day - but one day's slippage on tides was within the variation I'd planned"

"Pretty well ... variation? I'm aghast! You could've warned us!"

"Yeah as I say, I am sorry about that, but I felt you needed to be authentically angry with me to convince everyone else and to get the Elders to trust me."

"Well, I'm glad you're sorry - but you can stuff your apologies!" spluttered Luke.

Aldred, though, roared with laughter. "Brilliant! Absolutely brilliant. Wonderful plan and perfectly executed. I don't expect you to agree, Luke, and I understand you feel somewhat betrayed but .."

The sentence was interrupted by a roar in the distance. The not very far distance, actually.

"What the hell is that?" asked Luke.

"Bear - big, dangerous things. Claws, teeth, muscles. Not to be messed with. Quick, let's pack up - we're going to have to get out of here. I don't think our fire's going to stop it. Shame. Come on, let's get going.".

9 READY

Weeks passed. Horrible, mundane weeks which felt like every day was grinding along. Luke wondered at times if even life as Dung Man was better? At least there'd been breaks in the monotony and regular food every day. Normal food. Proper food.

There was some consolation that, after the first days, they had managed to get a regular fire going to make evenings warm and food more edible. Indeed on one occasion Aldred had almost jumped for joy as he discovered a certain mushroom which, once dried, was incredibly slow-burning and meant that as they travelled they could ensure a fire the next night too, without fiddling about with flints and starting from scratch every day!

Nevertheless, every day was about scraping a living: surviving and, frankly, surviving miserably. His clothes were coming apart and were filthy. His body was too, and he stunk. Even the occasional wash in a river failed to remove the smell, partly because the animal skin he now wore for extra heat was barely cured and smelt of rotting meat, but mostly, because he simply didn't have the energy spare to scrub clothes and body.

Nevertheless, Luke had stopped complaining. Stopped grumbling even, as that also took too much energy. And wasted energy meant potential failure to survive. Tougher, leaner and even meaner he returned to the camp they'd established now for a fortnight, at least relieved that they weren't constantly on the move as they had been at first. He was also much lighter on his feet as well as being much more aware of all that was going on around him. Even as he tuned into the conversation between Marsha and Aldred, his ears (not to mention a variation of Feeling) were scanning all the other noises and movement in the woods around him.

He could see that Marsha had scavenged a good range of tubers and a kind of wild onion, whilst Aldred had accrued a decent pile of wood that would easily last the night. With barely a sigh, he dropped the three rabbits he'd trapped and sat wearily (though with scarcely a sound) onto the ground. They'd eat well enough tonight and, since he was on third watch, he had every prospect of a decent sleep too. Such were the scant positives of 'freedom' he'd grown to grudgingly appreciate.

Aldred looked first at the rabbits and then, smiling warmly, at Luke himself. "I think you're ready," he said.

"Ready?" responded Luke. "Ready for what?"

Before Aldred replied, he reached forward and, taking one of the rabbits, started preparing it. Almost automatically, so did Luke. There were routines to survival and all shared them now. Skinning and gutting could continue while they talked.

"Ready for us to move on. On to the next stage," said Aldred eventually.

Luke's sulks, complaints and surly comments may have gradually lessened, but his essential inquisitiveness remained. He had learnt to temper his responses, and weeks of living in the wild had taught him patience. He continued to skilfully butcher the animal in his hands, wasting virtually nothing and carefully placing the waste on the leaves ready to dispose of them later without making a horrendous mess of the camp that had become their home. "Next stage?" he asked, after as long a gap as he could bear.

Aldred smiled approvingly again. "You don't think the goal of escaping from Coldharbour was to live like this, do you? We have a mission and I aim to complete it. But we couldn't even start if you were going to mess it all up with your youthful enthusiasm and ignorance of the Outland, as you call it. You'll need to know how to behave here."

"But I still know nothing about what it's like there in the villages and towns you told me about when we'd finished our dung rounds. You've taught me nothing about Outland."

"I've been teaching you and Marsha more basic stuff until now. Like how to survive, how to scratch a living in hiding and how to deal with nature's threats. When we first landed we had to run from everything. Remember that bear that first night? Now we'd drive it off, as we did that group of wolves last week. Now we're powerful and able to work as a team and think as a team. Now we're ready. Ready for the next stage."

"We? We're ready? What about Marsha? Is she ready?"

"Don't let your ego get too hurt but Marsha has been ready for some time. She's not as strong as you or I, but she's wily and a very quick learner. She's not got your hunting skills but she's got other strengths. Being different is good, though, because our various abilities complement each other's. Together we are a team, and a formidable one at that! Not only did she make the escape possible by her ingenuity, her presence now and in the future makes our chances of success that much higher."

"How do you rate our chances overall of succeeding?" asked Marsha with a laugh. A lovely laugh that, despite Luke's resentments and jealousies, he couldn't help finding just a little bit attractive. "And what are we aiming to succeed at anyway? All you've talked about for weeks has been survival. About keeping alive."

"You know full well there has always been more than that, and don't pretend you don't. You didn't risk your life to rescue us in order to live in a wood, scrabbling a living and digging holes to crap in."

"No she did it so she could live with two smelly men who smell worse than her!" laughed Luke.

"You know, Luke, that is the first proper laugh you've had since we left Coldharbour," Aldred said, with relief in his voice. "Proves I'm right. You're ready. You're both ready."

"Ready to find out what our Mage powers are and what we can do here in Outland?" asked Marsha incredulously? "You're not serious are you?"

"No, you're neither of you ready for that yet, I'm afraid. That's got to come at a later stage. But for now you're ready for us to move out of survival mode and get ready to integrate in those towns and villages. To mix with people."

"To what end?" asked Luke, now warming to the topic so much that he temporarily stopped work on the final rabbit. Aldred, though, noticed that the halt was mere moments long. Not only that, Luke's awareness was not diminished by his engagement with the conversation - an engagement that had been totally lacking since the escape. Yes, he was definitely ready at last.

"Our ultimate goal is to work with those I know who want to challenge the oppressive role of our beloved Emperor. But that's a long way down the road. Before that, and much more pressing, we must ensure Sharla's safe."

"Sharla? Who's Sharla?" asked Luke, as he and Aldred carefully threaded rabbit meat onto sticks and placed them over the (virtually smokeless) fire Marsha had built up more. She had finished preparing the tubers some time past and had placed them to cook more slowly around the outside of the fireplace.

Cooking, like much of woodland living, was a team activity, which continued almost without a need to talk about it. There were more important things to discuss.

"You'll remember I told you about a young girl with Mage powers that a Seeker encountered and hid?"

"Yes, of course. That was the reason you became a wanted man! I really am slow, sometimes!"

"Well in fairness, Luke, it was a detail in a long tale, and easily missed. Anyway, I couldn't bear the thought of what Magrat would do to her, so I rescued her and moved her to a place of safety. As far as I know she's still where I left her, as are others I would like to meet up with. There's unfinished business there as, like you, Sharla has gifts that were, I don't know, unusual."

"Like our so-called powers?" asked Luke, sarcastically.

"Not powers, Luke, gifts. Magery can be used for power play but it doesn't have to be so. In fact it's at its worst when used that way. That's why the Empire is so wrong, as it's based upon force and the use of power, rather than on appropriate use of gifts."

"But you told me that the 'ungifted' hated and killed the Mages. Didn't they need to use their abilities to protect themselves?"

"True, but it doesn't have to be so now. Especially if there are other abilities developing. We could develop a much better way of working and living together."

Marsha chuckled. "You're a real idealist, Aldred, aren't you? What makes you think a second order Mage like you can bring down the most powerful Empire in history?"

"Well, first, I'd correct your statement. The most powerful Empire in recent history it is. Past Empires of the Great Age were almost certainly much more powerful, and that was even without the abilities of magery. But to answer your question, I understand that changes can often be effected by smaller people, less powerful people. Especially when they work together. It is the weakness of the powerful that they actually think they can work alone."

"But you told us that Camrin and Magrat achieved what they did precisely by working together!" retorted Luke

"My point exactly, Luke! If two Mages can do so much together, just think what three Mages could manage. I've seen you two develop enormously as a team with me over our time together. We three - four if Sharla is, as I hope, still alive - plus others I can Seek and recruit, could, I believe, do so much. If I didn't think that, I'd've left you here months ago.

"You must understand that this is dangerous and risky and you need to be prepared to run and hide if you need to. To live like we have the last few months, keeping heads down, surviving."

"But first, you need to prepare us, in case we have to mix in with Outland people, so we don't stand out and get caught by Empire spies? Is that what you mean by the next stage?" enquired Marsha.

"Precisely my plan," replied Aldred. "And don't forget that one of your motivations in leaving Coldharbour was to seek a solution to their long-term problems."

"Yes, but how do they fit into the plan?" asked Marsha.

"To be honest, I'm not entirely sure," replied Aldred. "Some way down the road I think. For now it's one step at a time."

"So, if the next step is learning to assimilate into Outland society, when do we get to work out our powers? I mean our gifts?" asked a reenergised Luke.

Aldred smiled. "After that. As long as I can work out what those gifts are."

"Great," said Luke, "when do we start?"

"Well first I think we'd better do justice to these rabbits. Our supper looks ready to me."

10 ASSIMILATION TRAINING

The next two weeks were still hard. Wintertime in Coldharbour was always the toughest season but at least if they were back there, they would have stored up the harvested food and take the opportunity of lulls in stormy weather for trips out to catch fresh fish to augment the stored crops.

Here in the Outland, as Autumn developed in the woodland, the ground was already getting harder than normal, and making the gathering of tubers and other foods that could be obtained much tougher work. Game too was becoming scarcer, and the three renegades were competing with other hunters including wolves and bears.

However, Aldred had forged a formidable team who worked well together. Marsha had developed a sense for edible plants, and Luke had developed into a highly skilled hunter In the same way that he could sense shoals of fish below his boat, he could pinpoint animals long before they were aware of him. That gave him the edge both as a hunter of game and in avoiding those who'd seek to hunt him. Aldred, meanwhile had skills with tool- and weapon-making, not to mention the clever range of wooden pots and utensils he'd managed to make. Considering they had started off with a mere three metal knives, the well-equipped 'kitchen' at their base camp was highly impressive, and a huge step up from that first night's meal of torn deer meat, part-cooked over a crude fire.

Not only that, he was a great teacher of survival skills, sharing what he'd learnt during his time on the run alone. Thus, despite the challenges of approaching winter, the team survived. Better than that, they prospered. Aldred noticed that they had, to his surprise, put on weight over the time - weight in muscle, and toned muscle at that. Wild animals learned to steer clear of these new, powerful neighbours, who defended their territory forcefully and skilfully.

Better yet, there was a new-found energy in their activity. They had the reserves and the motivation to spend time talking, preparing and learning about Outland ways. The Coldharbour two even learnt to stop using language and terms (including 'Outland') which would give them away the moment they engaged with mainland folk. They would always risk standing out as strangers, but Aldred taught the two young people how to cover their strangeness with credible origins.

Aldred was now ready for them to move on, not just to the next stage, but for them to leave the deep woodland. The only thing they needed to make them properly blend in, however was going to be a real challenge. After all those weeks living rough, their clothing was hideous, guaranteed to provoke suspicion within moments of encountering any Southfleet inhabitants. Assimilation was going to be impossible without some clothes, and Aldred was coming to the conclusion that soon enough he'd have to admit he had no plan to deal with it.

In the meantime something more pressing was becoming necessary. A confession. And one that would undoubtedly not go down well. With plans for moving on well advanced, it was time for him to do the deed.

The last few days had been spent in completing the preparation of supplies for their travels. Marsha had discovered a large supply of remarkably nutritious fungi that they had been able to dry and pack, together with the smoked and dried meat they had accrued, plus some fruits and berries Marsha had collected. Aldred had made ingeniously constructed back packs out of animal skins and they had stowed all this food, wrapped in leaves and divided into daily portions.

Water was more of a problem, as the containers he had fashioned leaked slightly. Nevertheless, it was heavy and they would be limited as to how much they could carry, anyway. Fortunately, amongst Marsha's food-foraging skills she seemed to be gifted with an ability to sense the location of water, so Aldred was confident they would manage until they found the community where he hoped to find Sharla.

More pressing was his confession, and he could delay it no longer as they intended to set off on the morrow. Thus, as they sat down to eat their final meal in their woodland base, he shared with them his 'little problem.' Their problem, actually.

"Marsha and Luke, I need to tell you something before we set out tomorrow. You have both worked incredibly hard in preparing for the journey, after weeks of listening and learning and you deserve to hear what I am about to say."

Both the young people looked up earnestly. They had learnt amongst all their discoveries that Aldred was usually worth listening to, and they had developed a huge amount of respect for the older man. He was hoping that would continue after what he was about to share.

"You now know," he began, "so much about the way things work in the

Empire that I think you should be able to fit in. Our cover stories are pretty water-tight ..."

"Even if our water carriers aren't?" joked Luke.

"Indeed! Not only that, you're fully briefed about the evil ways of the Emperor and his government. I know you've only got my word on it and my opinions ..."

"Yes," interrupted Marsha, "but we got to question you quite deeply about all that. And I think we're both pretty sure we agree with you. We're a team, and we're ready to see what we can do against them."

"I'm grateful for that, Marsha. But we do have a problem. And I don't think you're going to like it when I tell you."

"Well we won't know, and neither will you, unless you share it, Aldred," cut in Luke.

"OK. Well as you know I promised that I would spend the last months looking and feeling and, I suppose 'tasting' your auras, to work out what gifts you have that make you the unique Mages that you clearly are."

"And?" said Luke

"And I have to say I, well, I still don't know."

"You what?" retorted a suddenly angry Luke. "You're trying to tell us that you, the all-wise Seeker, still haven't got a clue what we can do?"

"Well, apart from finding that your Feeling ability has a wider sensitivity than to tides and fish. Marsha, for example, also has her remarkable ability to sense whether food is edible, and where drinking water is. But the truth is: yes, I'm telling you that I've simply been unable to work out what else you can do."

"Brilliant! Brilliant!" shouted Luke, suddenly oblivious of the dangers of taking his senses away from constant monitoring of the surroundings or making unnecessary noises. "So we can defeat the Empire by steering boats and giving them food and drink? Absolutely brilliant! We've given up everything, faced a death sentence, lived all this time scratching to stay alive and that's all we can do? We'll sure give old Camrin a run for his money eh?"

"It's not that bad, Luke," said Marsha, hopefully.

"Yes it bloody is!" retorted Luke. "No actually, it's worse. It's blasted well hopeless! I thought ... I thought with our gifts we could combine and actually make all that sacrifice worthwhile."

"No it's not hopeless, Luke!" replied Aldred. "I promise you, there's some very powerful and effective magery in your makeup. I can feel it like you can Feel the sea and the wood of your boat or the presence of animals. It's just that, at the moment, can't work out what it is.

"When the first Porters discovered their gifts, it was most likely by accident. They wanted to throw something and forgot to pick it up first. Then they developed their ability further. Same with the Melders - you don't realise at first you're able to change what people are thinking and doing, until you do it. But we've been familiar with those abilities for generations now, and we Seekers are able to identify the ones with those recognisable gifts and tutor them in the ways of honing their skills."

"But in the meantime, oh wise and wonderful Seeker, we've got to sit around and face the wrath of the Empire until we have the good fortune to stumble on how we can fight it? Brilliant, I say again. And, and ..." but, lost for words Luke stormed off into the woods.

There was silence in the camp for a while until Aldred commented sardonically, "Well that went well."

"Five minutes to reverse five months of development," agreed Marsha, and shook her head sadly.

"So why aren't you storming off too?" he asked her.

"What would it achieve? Unless of course being angry would reveal what I can do? Anyway, as you say, it's not that you've found we can't do anything. It's just that as yet you haven't found out what we can do. That's different. You've found other people's gifts before, and hopefully you'll find ours too. Not only that, for me, being here is way better than living in Coldharbour. It was dull there, where I was 'just' a girl who was expected to grow up to do 'womanly' things. Since you arrived, my life had been much more interesting. I've always been a very sensible and pragmatic sort of person, which I think the ethos of Coldharbour sought to breed into its population. There wasn't much to aspire to for anybody, especially for the women, so we were ground down to comply.

"When I stumbled upon your conversations, I don't know, it was almost as if my horizons had lifted. I was OK with what I had. I was reconciled, I thought, with what the future offered ... and then, suddenly there was the possibility of something more. Something better? And, for all the struggles of the last months, I still feel there's the prospect of greater things to come. It's been harder work, for sure, but, all in all, I've actually been enjoying it. It's fun!"

Aldred laughed. He'd half expected Luke to react badly when told what he'd just shared, but he had definitely not expected to laugh! "You're a wonder, you are, Marsha. There's a lot more to you than I, or indeed poor Luke ever imagined. But you're right, it's not all dark and dim. And we won't be taking on Camrin and his cronies until we work out what's in our arsenal. Not to mention what Sharla can add to the pot!"

"Sorry, Aldred, another of those new words you use. 'Arsenal'?"

"Ah yes - it's a storehouse for weapons."

"So you are talking about power, not gifts this time?"

"To a degree, but only to a degree. Magery in recent times has been about using gifts as tools of power, but they can and should be used for so much more. I think that's one reason why poor Luke is so disappointed. I think he believes he will be made more special, just as Feeling made him so in Coldharbour."

"Don't worry too much about Luke. He's grown up a lot in these woods. He'll calm down in a while and look at it more reasonably. A bit more, hopefully!"

"I certainly hope so. I don't think I can cope with another interminable sulk!"

"Me neither," laughed Marsha and it wasn't long before Aldred was gently chuckling too.

11 SURPRISED

Luke did come back to the base after an hour or so, but there was little evidence he'd calmed down or was less sulky. He did, though, come back in time for his planned period of watch. And he did settle down for sleep reasonably peacefully after that when he was relieved by Marsha. However, when Aldred roused them at dawn for breakfast, he still had his old air of teenage sulkiness about him, and throughout their travels for the next days, his demeanour rarely lifted back to the cheerfully cooperative team member he'd become for the last few weeks.

They travelled mostly in a north-easterly direction for over a week, initially still remaining if possible in woodlands. Aldred explained that the original landing places Luke had identified would've made travel to the woods that had provided their safe haven for the winter very difficult as their route would have passed very near to villages that he knew were much more sympathetic to Empire spies than he would wish. The trouble now was that, in order to reach the remote village he was aiming for, they would be passing through some much more densely populated areas. However, avoiding them, would mean travelling many more miles than he felt they could manage, not to mention the extra time it would take. With luck, their acquired stealth would get them through and, with a bit more good fortune, they would not run into anyone who would pose a threat.

"Perhaps 'Luck' is our secret ability!" responded Luke, sarcastically.

Luck, though is a two-edged sword and what seemed initially to be terribly bad luck, transpired to be a stroke of good fortune in the end.

As the woods thinned out, they needed to be much more aware of the possibility of being seen from afar. Sometimes, when there was a village nearby, they travelled through the night to avoid the possibility of encountering folk. They developed crafty journeying techniques - never standing on rises, traversing hillsides without reaching the top so that bracken and trees would always provide cover for example.

Then, at one point they were forced to travel along a long escarpment with steep cliff sides on either edge. It was that or descend all the way to the bottom, pass along an equally narrow valley, and then be forced to climb again at the far end.

It seemed worth the risk but, after an hour or so, as it narrowed increasingly, they realised that the route had a very well-worn path, one that looked decidedly as if it were regularly used by people and not animals.

Aldred had barely suggested that they take especial care and be ready to run back, when suddenly Luke became aware of animals ahead of him. Previously his gift of awareness had been restricted to sensing life in general, but with practice he had honed his abilities to discriminate between various lifeforms in the woods. Though he had tested himself, he had proved unable to sense his companions, so had assumed that he could not identify humans. But as he pulled up and sought to work out what was approaching them, he had a strong feeling that what was coming was walking upright - and coming quickly.

His heart beating strongly, he whispered a sharp warning to Aldred and Marsha. "Quick, we need to hide. There's a group of people coming and there's no time to turn tail. Now! Over there by those rocks."

It was a poor place to hide, but the only option available: two large rocks with a small ledge behind them. The three of them could barely all squeeze in, though at least there were handholds so they didn't fall backwards down the sheer cliff face beneath them. If those approaching carried on at their current speed and passed on by quickly, with luck they would not be noticed.

Such luck could be wished for, but was not forthcoming.

Barely had they secreted themselves, when a horde of armed men crashed out of the undergrowth and initially they did look likely, as had been hoped, to be passing on by. Unfortunately one of the men shouted, as he reached the clearing near the rocks, that he needed to relieve himself. Several others chorused their need too and the commander - a large fellow with a helmet sporting a red feather on top - called the march to a halt and gave them five minutes to do their business.

Where else would twenty-five men relieve themselves but against the large rocks inviting them so to do?

"Oh please," muttered Luke to himself, "please don't let them see us!" And, shutting his eyes he trembled in fear as he repeated endlessly to himself, "Don't let them see us," expecting at any moment a shout of alarm as one of the soldiers spied and dragged them out. But time passed and no shouts arose.

Still muttering his incantation, he could no longer resist opening an eye to look. Not only were the soldiers not seeing them, as he looked sideways he saw one joker who had decided to stand on the edge of the cliff and pee dramatically downwards. To Luke's absolute horror, the showman turned directly towards his face and met him eye to eye. Barely a metre away yet, miraculously and impossibly, he did not see Luke! He looked directly past him and shouted to another humorist, mirroring his actions on the other side of the rocks ... who didn't see them either!

Still locked in fear and tension, the three travellers stood unmoving until the soldiers finished their toileting and recommenced their route march. Five minutes or more passed before Aldred chuckled gently and suggested they might move to safer positions and get the hell off the escarpment before any more soldiers arrived. It took an hour at least, though, before any of them spoke after that.

Once off the final, even narrower part of the escarpment, they turned north-east and clambered as quickly as possible, to get out of sight and out of what they now realised was a main travelling route. Looking at it from this perspective it became obvious why the troop had taken the same route as they had taken. There was clearly no alternative that was passable and, despite the encounter, they were at least reassured that it had been unavoidable.

Once settled, deep in the woods, Marsha remarked how strange it was that, though she and Luke had grown up in a place with virtually no mature trees, she now found herself feeling deeply peaceful when surrounded by such massive trunks. "Perhaps we have grown used to associating them with safety and security?" he responded.

It was a rare moment of unanimity which helped to heal the recent divisions a little, plus break the silence resulting from their frightening encounter behind the rock.

As they looked around, they assessed that, unlike the escarpment, this was not somewhere where people travelled frequently. There were a number of light paths suggesting animal runs, but nothing else. There was also plenty of dry wood to gather and when Marsha, found them a gently running river, they decided to settle there for the night by its banks. Luke even decided it might be a good spot to catch some fish so, while the other two set up camp, he waded around gently seeking some supper, with remarkable success.

Though he found river fish (Aldred informing him these were called trout) somewhat less to his taste than those from the sea, Luke said he was more than delighted not to be eating smoked, dried deer or rehydrated mushrooms for once! It also made him feel better to be useful, though in truth it didn't lighten his mood significantly, especially given the sense of confusion caused by recent events.

Once the fish were gutted and cooking nicely on one of the ingeniously smokeless fires Aldred had taught them, Luke could hold back no longer. "Aldred," he started, "how the hell didn't those guys see us? They looked me straight in the eyes and still missed me!"

Aldred had been expecting the question of course, but he had no definite answer, and after their last conversation, was dreading it. "Truth is, Luke, I don't properly know. But I do know it was you who did it."

"Him?" asked a suddenly intrigued Marsha. "How? I thought they'd have us for certain and then, no, off they went!"

"How? I'm afraid is something I don't know. But who? That I am sure of! As we hunched behind those rocks, I felt an initial surge of an aura around Luke, just like he projected when he was Feeling through the Curve. Somehow he hid us. Somehow he made us unseen."

"I made us invisible? However did I do that? Pretty good trick if I could remember how I did it! To be honest, I can't remember doing anything, just hunkering down and hoping against hope that they missed us."

"Maybe that was all it took?" mused Aldred. "I mean, how do you make Feeling work, or seeking for animals? And while we're on that gift, how did you know it was Camrin's Corps coming and not wolves?"

Marsha interrupted, intrigued. "How did you know it was his elite troops?"

"The Commander's red feather was the sign. Vicious bunch and rather unnerving. I've never seen them so far from the capital. Worrying, but we can consider that later. Right now, I need to know what you did, Luke? How did you shield us? That's a very neat trick and one that could prove useful."

But Luke was not impressed. "You're not going to get around me that easily. I'm still really irritated with you, and you're not going to get me back on your side by pretending you're impressed with being invisible. It's cool, but just another way of running away and hiding. It's almost like being a coward! I can see through your flattery."

"No, honestly, it could be a good skill, as is the ability to sense out people. Using both, today is not only impressive in itself, it's also jolly useful! Being able to hide not only yourself, but us all is, frankly, remarkable! I've never encountered anything like it. You're proving more intriguing and more mysterious by the day!"

When Luke still didn't seem convinced, Marsha added another thought. "Actually, it's better even than that. We weren't just unseen, we were unnoticed. They didn't even notice how much we stink! We haven't had a decent wash in months and these skins are rotting really badly. They ought to have been able to smell us halfway across the valley. Yet they didn't even get a sniff. Seriously, Luke, tell Aldred: what was it you did?"

Marsha's interest was enough to ensure that the conversation continued and, as she listened more, she was fascinated by the level of detail that Aldred sought in Luke's actions, his thoughts and the words he'd used to achieve what had been the most perplexing of miracles. He'd previously said that a part of a Seeker's function was to train new Mages to utilise their gifts to the maximum. Obviously with a new ability, he needed to learn more himself first.

Then, later, after supper and before they settled down for the night, Aldred persuaded Luke to practice being unnoticed; with varying degrees of success, as it took some time before Luke could recreate his actions. It turned out that if someone could already see Luke before he sought to be invisible, then it simply didn't work. But, even if they knew exactly where he was, but had turned away as he became, as they now named it, 'Unseen,' then, sure enough they could not detect him. Amazingly, if he then walked up to them and touched them, they could feel him, but still not see him.

However, Luke's ability to move or speak, once unnoticed was variable. Sometimes he could, but at other times he was unable to manage it. Aldred suggested that, perhaps Luke's ability to concentrate was an issue, which of course Luke took as a criticism and the evening which had started so positively began to go downhill again.

"I think we've done enough for tonight," Aldred eventually decided. "You've done well. We've all done well, but I think we've done enough for now. Marsha's on first watch and I'm on second, so you'll get a good night's sleep. You've earned that at least, Luke. Not least because I owe you my life after today. You really did do well and I am grateful. Thanks."

Sometimes a little gift of graceful gratitude can act as a peace-inducing balm, and Luke smiled gently in response, for the first time in weeks. Knowing it was some hours until his own watch duties, he curled up and went to sleep.

After some time staring gently at the fading fire, Aldred said, quietly, "Marsha?"

"Yes, Aldred?"

"There's something else I haven't said about today's episode."

"Which is?"

"You two are such an anomaly Mage-wise that I seem to be re-learning my own skills all over again."

"You've said something similar before, I think?"

"Indeed! And I suspect I will say it again."

"So what is the 'something else' you wanted to share? Something to share with me and not with Luke, I suspect?"

"Again, Marsha, you can perceive more than edible tubers! But yes it is about you … and … and I don't know how to handle Luke on this, but, when he was doing his 'invisibility' trick, he wasn't the only one involved."

"What do you mean? Someone else was doing something?"

"Yes, Marsha, and it was you!"

"Me? I didn't do anything at all, apart from stand stock-still in terror!"

"No, I think you're right. You weren't consciously doing anything, but your aura was exhibiting some sort of activity? It was almost as if you were adding, augmenting or accentuating what Luke was enacting. It was the same when he was practising earlier. Something was happening around you too, perhaps as you sought to encourage, or will him on. Indeed, when you

51

went off gathering into the woods, that coincided with a period when Luke's performance dipped somewhat. He could still do it, but not so well"

"You've said that Mages work together in other work, haven't you?"

Oh yes, that is true, but that is when they are all doing the same thing. Magrat and Camrin's pet Mages are all, intentionally, low-level so they don't threaten their hegemony. So they need several Mages in conjunction to keep them in power."

"Ok, but didn't you say the couple have different powers and work together sometimes?"

"Yes, but that's doing different things, at the same time, the same way groups banded together during the Mage Wars. What seems to be happening with you and Luke is quite new. It's a sort of synergy. You're sort of both doing different things, but in the process working together to make, I suppose, a joint effect?"

"Teamwork-magery, maybe?"

"Exactly! It's something I've not encountered before. It'll be really great, no, essential, to explore this together so you, too, can hone your skills. I just don't know how to broach the topic with Luke."

"So, what is the problem with just telling him?"

"He's struggling enough with feeling that his gifts aren't that impressive in the first place. I'm not sure how he'll react when he finds out that he needs someone else to make them work better?"

"I think you're underestimating him, Aldred. Luke is still childish in some ways, but I've seen him mature and develop in our time together. He needs time to adapt to new things and new ideas, but he can learn to work things through and sort them out, eventually. I'm hopeful he will eventfully outgrow his sulks."

"And you call me an idealist!" chuckled Aldred.

"We'll see. We'll see," said Marsha with a gentle smile. "For now, it's my watch and you'll need some sleep. Don't spend too much snooze time wondering how you're going to tell him. The moment will come!"

"I'm adding patience to your list of gifts, Marsha."

"Sleep well, Aldred."

12 ATTACK

The following week was arduous. Long days travelling over difficult terrain, trying always to avoid inhabited places, which of course meant the roughest, toughest landscapes. The fear of meeting Camrin's Corps was, after their narrow escape, always in their minds.

Nevertheless, as the ground became more mountainous, they couldn't help but admire the incredible views and sheer vastness of the mainland. For folk who had been contained in such a small and limited area as Coldharbour, Marsha and Luke were overawed by the size of the land around them. After the weeks of travelling, even from high hillsides, they could no longer see the coastline from which they had set out and as they stood looking across the vista below them, Luke shivered and whispered, "It makes you feel very small, doesn't it, Marsha?"

"It does. I never dreamed being here would or could be so huge."

"And you can barely see a tiny proportion of it," added Aldred. "Mind you, before the seas rose, we understand there was so very much more land. And, of course many, many more people. There is evidence of huge areas where people lived closely together. They reckon millions died because of the wars, the effects of the explosions and because most people had no idea of supporting themselves without their mersheens and teck. Many probably just starved. Think how hard it was for us to survive when first we landed, and that was with my experience to aid us."

"It must've been horrible," said Marsha. "Couldn't they use their teck to stop the climate changing and the water levels rising?"

"Maybe, but quite probably it was their teck in the first place that changed the weather patterns, we believe."

"Oh come on," said Luke, "how could human action change the weather? We're too small to make a difference, surely?"

"Possibly, but who knows, maybe they believed that too. And believed it wrongly! Each person might have been small but the effects of their lifestyles, added together, changed so much. Or so we believe. And by the time they'd discovered what they'd done, it was too late and they found they couldn't reverse it.

"Anyway, I'm pleased to say that we're not too far from the village we've been heading for, and we've managed to get this far without needing to blend in with proper clothing. That was really worrying me when we set off, but somehow our other challenges have turned out to be more important. Never mind, we're nearly there now and we can get some new clothing there, hopefully. Let's crack on today and we might even get to Abbas by nightfall. Assuming they're still where they were."

"What do you mean by that?" said a suddenly worried Luke. "Why shouldn't they be?"

"It's been over a year, and a whole village keeping its locality and its people hidden is some challenge, even in an area as remote as this on the edge of the Empire. Especially as Camrin's Corps are about. These are dangerous times."

So they continued along the sides of often steep and rugged hillsides, trying very hard to blend into the background. As they travelled, Luke practised his shielding techniques, never very sure whether they were unnoticed or not. Eventually, they descended a hill onto gently undulating grasslands, enabling them to pick up their pace a little. It was a warm, balmy day and they were feeling really positive. Their mood, though, was overoptimistic and disaster was about to strike!

Luke had relaxed his shielding, in the mistaken belief that they were sufficiently hidden by the long grassland they were now travelling through. Walking was hard enough as it was, without the additional effort of shielding them.

The grass, however, also hid a hunting group of large cats and, in his weariness, he had also stopped scanning ahead for lifeforms. As so often, it is when you are near your destination that your guards go down!

Fortunately, his unconscious senses kicked in, though late, just in time to shout a warning and Aldred, who was in the lead, managed to duck just as the first cat leapt at him. Instead of felling him as intended, the beast caught his arm with its claws, giving the travellers just enough time to draw their weapons and start fending off the attack.

However, the cats were canny and experienced hunters, even if they weren't used to fighting armed humans. There hadn't been enough time to organise and the three humans soon found themselves separated from each other, hacking desperately and fleeing in terror. Luke dispatched one very large cat, but not without sustaining severe cuts on his right leg. He was also having to deal with three more of the hissing, crafty animals.

The last he saw of Aldred was him backing off as two cats sought to attack him from two sides at once. Marsha, meanwhile, fortunately only had one assailant to contend with and she appeared to be managing well, since the cat seemed cautious and a little hesitant. However, she was also being forced to move further and further from her companions.

A larger group of cats might well have succeeded in their attack on Luke, but he was now confident that, with his senses now fully operational, he could deal with his foes, eventually. They only had sight and sound, while he reasoned his additional senses would even out the battle.

He backed carefully towards a large bush and, correctly predicting their movements, almost before they knew themselves, he dived, turned and killed one leaping cat, rolling over as he did, cleanly pulling his spear from the cat's body.

Then, before the second one could leap, Luke continued his roll, and ducked behind the bush. Momentarily out of sight, he hunkered down, shut his eyes and made himself Unseen. Barely daring to breathe, he opened his eyes, stood up, slowly backed up a little and calmly waited for the cats. Confident now of their prey, the two approached simultaneously from either side of the bush and then stopped, perplexed to see no one there. When one cat suddenly collapsed with a fatal gash upon his side, the second thought for a second of turning tail in terror. But it was a second too long, as Luke's spear stabbed viciously in his throat.

Exultant but fearful for his companions, Luke concentrated hard on keeping his shields in place as he ran back in the direction of Aldred. The older man had succeeded in mortally wounding one of the big cats, which lay mewing as it died, but the other feline had managed to get him onto the ground. Aldred was rolling on the ground with the beast, trying desperately to keep the snarling head off his own throat. However, his strength was clearly failing fast.

Luke only had seconds and could not reach the battling pair in time, so he threw his spear at the cat.

Weeks of hunting had improved his accuracy and the weapon sunk deep into the beast's chest killing it instantly. As it collapsed, its body almost crushed poor Aldred, until Luke ran up, rolled the cat off his friend and reclaimed his spear.

"Quick," he said, "get your breath back and let's find Marsha."

Aldred got up as quickly as he could, retrieved his own weapon from where he had dropped it in his struggles and, dabbing the blood on his arm, looked around. "Where is she? Where did you see her last?" he asked, desperately?

"Over there. She was backing off in that direction. Her cat didn't seem to be as aggressive as ours, but she's smaller than either of us and she's only got a long knife. I can sense the thing, but it's some way off now. Come on!"

The two set off as fast as they could, frantic to catch up with the girl. So focused on looking as far ahead as possible, they failed to see a sudden dip, hidden by grass. Walking slowly they would have noticed it, no doubt, but at high speed, they tumbled uncontrollably downwards and fell deep into a ditch. For Luke all went suddenly black.

13 TRUST

Luke opened his eyes and all he could feel was pain. His head ached, his eyes were muzzy and he seemed to be lying at the bottom of a deep ditch. Worse than that, his leg hurt mightily and he moaned aloud.

"Oh good, I thought you were out for the night," said a relieved Aldred. "How are you feeling? I've been pressing on your leg and I think I've stopped the bleeding, but I think your other leg may be broken. Does it hurt?"

"Hurt? It's bloody agony! Where the hell are we, and how did we get here?"

"You're not going to like the answer."

"I don't like anything at the moment. But let's get out of this place, and catch up with Marsha."

"That's not going to be easy, I'm afraid."

"Why not? Once we're out of this ditch I could use my spear as a crutch. I'd be slow but ..."

"It's not a ditch. It's a trap. We're caught in a tunnel trap, dug by giant creatures that will be coming to eat us in a few hours. We do need to get out, but only one of us can do so. I'll need you to help me climb out - it's too high on my own."

"Giant creatures? First cats, then, what? What sort of 'creatures'?"

"They're like spiders. Huge great horrible things. I don't know how they got to be so big, but I've encountered them before. You need to help me out, and I'll bring someone back to rescue you."

"I don't believe you. I've never heard of giant spiders. You've never mentioned them before and you never warned us ..."

"True, but I've never seen them this far west. They're quite common in the badlands and ... look, this is wasting time. Why are you being difficult? It's our only option."

"You could help me out, and I'll get assistance. I don't trust you. You've done nothing but lie to us, deceiving us into getting arrested and forcing us to leave our homes. You're just after my Marsha. I've seen the way you look at her. You ..."

Aldred's patience broke at this point. "Luke, just hear yourself and shut up, will you? You're acting like a big kid. Half an hour ago you were a mighty warrior, using your gifts in combination, dispatching four hungry lions. You've just saved my life. Of course I'm coming back! And for what it's worth, no, I'm not interested in Marsha, and unless you help me out, there won't be time to get out and back to save you, too. You need to get me out. And soon!"

"I'll just hide. I'll be Unseen. You're just worried about yourself and your precious skin. You don't care about me. Or Marsha, actually!"

"Luke, these spiders come out at night because they can't see. They work by feel rather than sight or smell, so being Unseen won't help you. Please, help get me out! I promise I'll come back for you."

"I don't trust you."

"Faith is like that, son. Can you remember the first time you shut your eyes and had total confidence in the Feeling to guide you through the twists and turns of the Curve?"

"I remember it like it was yesterday."

"Can you remember, though that someone with experience and authority encouraged you to trust yourself, to trust your training, trust all you'd learnt, trust your teacher and, more than anything, to trust yourself?"

"That's almost exactly what happened!"

"And it worked, didn't it?"

"Well, yes ..."

"And it's what's happened here, too. We've worked together as a team. I've encouraged you and trained you, and you know, if you look deep into your heart, that all I have done has made you a better person. And I've never intentionally brought you harm, have I?"

"Not intentionally, no. But ..."

"This attack came out of the blue, son. We jointly let our guards down and now we're all paying a big price for it. But it's not hopeless. With all my experience I can see a way out. But for that, you're just going to have to trust me. I won't let you down. I can't absolutely promise I can save us, but I absolutely promise I will do everything I can to get us help. The village of Abbas, which we're heading for is really quite near. They'll have fire to chase away the creatures and ropes to get you out. Trust me, please?"

Luke was silent for a minute or two then, "OK. Come on, let's get it done.

It took more time than they had imagined - the edge was barely in reach if Aldred climbed up on Luke's shoulders, which was a task in itself. Twice they fell over, and Aldred was beginning to despair. As he lay trying to get his breath back, he did consider if staying and fighting would be an option, but he'd seen these creatures before. And even if they survived a night, they'd still be stuck in the tunnel, with more of the horrors to come the following night.

One more enormous effort and he had a bit of luck. When he reached out he saw a sizeable bush on the lip that he could grab and pull himself out by, all the while praying madly that he didn't uproot it. He did but fortunately he had one leg over the edge by that point and he was able to clamber over it and get out.

He barely stopped to get his breath back. Time was running out. He leant over and promised once more he'd be back as soon as he could.

"Better do, too!" muttered Luke.

Time passed and Luke began to worry. A part of him didn't really believe the spider story, but most of him very much feared it was true and, as he looked up and saw the sky gradually darkening, he began to worry more. Where was he? Why wasn't Aldred back? How far was this village?

And then a surprising thought, as he wondered if Marsha was OK. Where did those accusations he'd flung at Aldred come from? He hadn't had romantic thoughts about Marsha for months now. She was dirty and smelly these days (though admittedly, so was he!), she'd hacked her lovely hair off to make it manageable. She was not at all the feminine, attractive girl he'd admired in Coldharbour. What was worse, she was so blasted smug and able these days, always right and always, always agreeing with Aldred.

Yet, somehow, when he thought about her, he felt a pleasant warmness. He also felt a deep concern about her, which was somehow not only surprising, it was also a jolly sight more pleasant than thinking about giant spiders, or the pain in his leg.

The light continued to fade away, though, and Luke began to become aware of a gentle clicking noise to his right. Life-sensing wasn't helping him to gauge the distance, because the tunnel curved slightly as it got further away, but eventually he realised that something had rounded the corner and was coming in his direction. Something very big and dark.

"You chose a fine time to tell the truth, Aldred," he muttered and put all his efforts into being Unseen. "You never know," he muttered, "Aldred doesn't know everything." But he wasn't feeling optimistic.

Closer and closer the horrific dark shape approached as the clicking got gradually nearer.

Luke tensed himself and looked as intensely as he could in the minimal light for a target for his spear. He reckoned he'd probably only have one go, and had to make it count first time. An eye? The mouth? He wasn't sure though he was certain that again Aldred had been right. The massive beast nearly filled the tunnel, and would certainly feel him as it passed along.

Then an idea suddenly flashed into his mind, just before the spider reached him. He struggled to his feet and then dived under those feelers

59

dragging and clicking below its dark and horrific mouth. As his momentum took him, he twisted round onto his back and then, with all the effort he could muster, thrust his spear upwards into the creature's unprotected head parts. The monster reared in agony, flipped around and fled, clearly injured and dragging its body as it went. It wouldn't be back, which was good. Very good, and a huge relief.

What was bad was that in its spasms it had wrenched Luke's spear from his hand, and left him now unarmed. His damaged leg hurt like crazy too, and, what was worse, Luke could now hear clicking again. This time on his left.

Part 3 - Marsha

14 OUTCAST

Marsha backed off slowly. She could see that the cat, though large, was smaller than the others and, judging by its hesitancy, less experienced. It had probably made a tactical error in following her, its head turned by greed and the excitement of the chase. Three targets was more than they had caught in weeks, and the feline would have been more effective joining in with one of the other groups attacking Aldred or Luke. But it was here now, getting farther from the others and, as Marsha could see, it was still mighty dangerous, perfectly capable of overpowering her, especially since she was armed only with a large knife.

However, the weapon glinted threateningly, having already inflicted a painful cut early on in their encounter. The juvenile cat was taking no chances, aiming to wear Marsha down, feint, lunge and, at the right moment, pounce. It clearly had enough experience for that approach.

Marsha, meanwhile, found herself gradually moving farther and farther from her companions and feeling very exposed. She hoped, though, that the small copse of trees nearby might give her some advantage, providing something to work around in her manoeuvres.

The stalemate was eventually broken when she heard a slight noise to her right amongst the trees. Fearing there might after all be another cat joining her assailant, she took her eye slightly off the animal. A near fatal mistake, as the cat, sensing her distraction chose that moment to leap, fortuitously knocking her blade from her hand at the same time. Panic rose in Marsha as she struggled to hold the fang-filled head away from hers, whilst the pain of its claws started to bite into her chest. Mustering all her strength, she fought valiantly against her foe, but knew her chances were fading. Keeping the weight of those jaws away was getting harder and harder. Any second might be her last.

Then, suddenly the beast gave a surprised grunt, slumped on her and then stopped moving. Fearing suffocation, desperation filled her, and she managed to garner just enough of her fast-diminishing strength to roll it off her.

Marsha scrambled over desperately, jumped to her feet and dived to retrieve her weapon, ready to face a further onslaught. But the cat just lay unmoving. Then she saw why: sticking out of the cat's side was a large, crude arrow. Relieved and perplexed in equal measure, for neither Aldred nor Luke had a bow amongst their weapons, Marsha looked around desperately to see who or where her mysterious saviour was.

"Are you alright?" asked a hesitant voice, as a tall young man appeared from amongst the trees. "And is it dead?"

"It certainly looks it." she replied. "That was one hell of a good shot!"

"Lucky, I'd say. I haven't hit any of the last ten animals I've shot at. But mighty glad that one scored."

He walked closer and, after examining the dead cat, retrieved his arrow, muttering something about it being a shame the meat wasn't palatable. He then held out his hand towards her, an action that left Marsha confused initially, until she remembered her orientation lessons with Aldred. Recalling that this was a way of greeting new people and perhaps indicating that they were no threat, she responded likewise, and shook hands for the first time in her life. "I'm Callan, by the way." he added, "I don't recognise you from Abbas. Where are you from?"

Marsha took a sharp intake of breath, and responded excitedly, "You're from Abbas? Is it near? That's where I'm heading. Can you take me there?"

"It's not far," replied Callan, "but no, I can't take you there. It's too dangerous for me."

"It can't be more dangerous than being attacked by killer cats," laughed Marsha.

"For you maybe, but even more so for me. If I return they'd kill me for certain. Anyway, the village itself was abandoned some weeks back after the last raid in the area from Camrin's Corps. They were getting too close and might've stumbled upon it, even though it's mighty well hidden. Otherwise, I probably wouldn't be telling you, since you're a stranger. In fact if I wasn't in shock from actually hitting something with my bow, I wouldn't have even mentioned the place. But in those, um, original clothes, I did think you were unlikely to be an Empire spy! Don't they know how to cure leathers where you come from?"

And he joined her laughter. It was the first time in months that Marsha had laughed so much, such was her relief. And Callan had a nice face, an honest look about him. She felt instinctively that she could trust him.

"Well, perhaps you could come back to my friends with me? They were being attacked by the rest of these beasts, and they might welcome your archery skills too. I came from over there," she added, pointing back towards the place where they were initially attacked, realising suddenly quite how far she had travelled while holding the cat at bay.

Callan, though, was hugely reluctant to head in that direction, and it took considerably more entreaty for Marsha to eventually persuade him to accompany her. First he said he couldn't mix with Abbas folk, then he told some fanciful tale of a monster spider ditch they would have to avoid. Finally he complained it was getting late, dark and dangerous. Indeed, it was only when she said she'd happily go without him that he changed his intransigence, indicating that he was not by nature one who enjoyed being alone. Having finally found company, even dishevelled and stinking as Marsha was, he obviously felt reluctant to lose it.

They set off but found nothing at all, except the bodies of the remaining cats. "Your companions must be mighty warriors to have dispatched so many of these creatures," he said in awe. "I'm incredibly glad the cats never found me. I've been living here for weeks now, and I would've been easy prey for them!"

"That's as may be, Callan, but right now I'm more interested in finding my friends. I can't imagine where they have gone!"

Callan was about to reply when he suddenly tensed and grabbed Marsha's arm, pulling her down low. "What the ...?" she started to say, but he just put his hands over her mouth and begged her, desperately, to be quiet. "There are some folk from Abbas coming up the hill. Please, we need to go. I need to go - they will kill me. Please. Make no noise. If you want to stay with them then do, but I need to go. Now!"

His obvious fear, together with the fact that they had not found Aldred and Luke, made Marsha's mind up for her, and together the two of them crawled as fast as they could until they were past a hump that obscured them from their adversaries. Then they ran as fast as they could.

Once she felt it was safe enough to do so, she asked Callan where they were going. "I have a sort of camp in that wood where we first met. It's not much. I'm a village boy and not used to living off the land. But it's pretty secure."

"Any food?" she asked without much hope of a positive reply. Her expectations were more than matched! However, as they walked through the trees, she saw a fair number of plants that she knew had good, tasty roots and collected a decent amount of edible fungi and fruit too. They wouldn't starve that night. She ensured Callan collected some firewood too, and filled his helmet with water as they crossed a stream.

They finally came to a small clearing before a steep, craggy cliff and Callan sheepishly announced they had arrived, pointing to a pile of stones from an old rock-fall which, as they got closer turned out to hide the entrance to a decent-sized cave.

"Actually," said Marsha, rather approvingly, "this is a lot better than I had expected. I've slept in much worse places in the last few months, I can tell you. And look over there - some flints! We can have a fire too!" She then settled down to starting a fire and preparing a filling and tasty meal.

Callan was very impressed. "I haven't seen fire for weeks, and I've only lived on raw meat and a few berries for all that time. This is amazing! You have no idea how grateful I am that my arrow shot true earlier. I was almost ready to give in, hand myself over to the Abbas folk and take the consequences. It would've been better to die quickly than starve to death."

***

Later, when they had fed and settled down, Marsha could ask the question that had been burning on her lips since she had met him. "Whatever did you do to make them want to kill you so badly?" she asked.

"Nothing. And everything!" he responded, then added, "It's complicated. Have you ever been in love?"

"Not really, but how is that relevant?" she replied.

"Well, I lost my heart to one of the Abbas village girls, but my attentions weren't welcomed by her father. He thought he could do better for her than the tanner's apprentice," he added bitterly.

"How about by the girl herself?"

"Ah well, actually Portha seemed quite interested I think, but her father didn't want her or me to be interested in each other. First of all he was just rude to me but later on he started to threaten me that if I didn't keep away from his little girl, he'd beat me up. He was a big bloke, massive arms, being the blacksmith and all. I couldn't really argue."

"So what happened then?"

"One day Portha was found all bruised and crying by one of her neighbours, and before anyone could work out what happened, her father Brusca came home and dragged her back into their home. When he came out, he announced that I had beaten her up, trying to force myself upon her, and that she was too distressed to talk to anyone. It was my bad luck to be just around the corner when the mob came looking for me, convincing them that I was nearby because of a recent encounter with Portha."

"And had you done it?" Marsha asked. She was a little worried, but to be honest she felt in her bones that this ineffectual and rather gentle man really didn't seem capable of such a heinous crime.

"Of course not!" he said, angrily, "I hadn't been near her for weeks! Not seen her or talked to her, leave alone have a chance to be alone with her. I wouldn't do that. I couldn't do that! You must believe me!"

"You know, strangely, I do, Callan. That's terrible for you. And for her, of course. But what did she say?"

"Well, they took her out of their home, in front of everyone and Brusca demanded she tell everyone the 'terrible thing' I'd done to her."

"And did she?"

"Not at first. Initially she just stood there, looking at the floor and crying. But then he shook her and shouted at her to tell everyone that I had tried to rape her. "Tell them it was him! Tell them!" he kept saying, until she eventually nodded, and that was that! They dragged me off to beat me up and kill me and… and well, that would have been the end, except Dorcas arrived and wanted to know what was going on. She told them we were in enough danger of being discovered, without a riot giving us away to the Empire!"

"Who is Dorcas?"

"Sorry, Dorcas is the Chief Elder of the village and …"

"But Dorcas is a woman's name, Callan!"

"So? She is a woman."

"You have a woman as Chief Elder?"

"Of course. Why not? She's the cleverest and the wisest. She's canny and tactical and a better sword fighter than anyone else. Why wouldn't a woman be Chief Elder?"

"You know, I can't give you one reason, Callan. It's just where I come from, it just would never happen."

"Where do you come from, Marsha?"

"I'll tell you later. For now, finish your story."

So Callan told how Dorcas listened to Brusca's accusations, and everyone agreed that Portha had confirmed Callan's guilt. "However, she said they didn't execute people in Abbas. It was wrong. The sort of thing the Empire did and not an Abbas thing. Brusca was furious but Dorcas stuck to her decision and said I had to leave. What I'd done was terrible and against justice, but that she would not do something equally wrong. Something about two wrongs not making a right.

Instead, she gave me an hour to get out of the village, after which if I was ever seen by Abbas folk, they could do what they liked. Brusca kept saying that I'd run right to the Empire and tell them where we were, but she said I didn't know where the people of Abbas were heading imminently, as even he didn't.

"So I ran. And ran, until I found these woods. Fortunately I'd grabbed my bow and arrows as I went past my father's home, or I would have starved by now. But I do think that I wouldn't have lasted very much longer. I've had little luck with hunting, I've never had to survive in the wild, and running into you has been the first bit of luck I've had in weeks. You do believe me, don't you? You're not worried you're sharing a cave with a rapist?"

"Even if I am," she said with a smile on her face, "I'm not threatened. I'm stronger and faster than you. So if you even try, I'll kill you without a second's hesitation."

Callan looked at her uncertainly. He wasn't sure, despite the smile, if she were joking and rapidly came to the conclusion she might just mean it! He was certainly no fighter, and she definitely looked tough enough to better him.

He smiled uncertainly. When she did too, it felt like an implicit agreement that both felt safe together, and they talked long into the night. Marsha told at least an outline of her story of Coldharbour, Luke and Aldred, promising there would be time for the detail later. For tonight they needed some sleep and could take it turns to keep watch - a concept Callan found novel, but didn't disagree with. Marsha settled the fire down to stop it smoking as it got lower, and took first watch.

However it had been a long and tiring day and, for the first time since their escape from Coldharbour, she dropped off while on guard duty. Callan did wake up at one point and noticed that she hadn't woken him but, used to having to risk sleeping anyway, he just snuggled down again, glad to have a companion after weeks of loneliness and barely existing. Maybe, as he'd said, his luck was changing after all.

15 REBUILD

The next weeks were disappointing and exciting in equal proportions. Despite several sorties out of the woods to try to find Luke and Aldred, they found no signs of them at all, which was a massive blow to Marsha. She had left her home, dramatically rescuing her friend and his companion, and now she was stuck in the middle of nowhere in Outland, with someone she hardly knew, and living with the slight uncertainty of his rape accusation hanging in the air. She had no idea what to do next. Her only plan had been, if separated to go to Abbas, which she now knew had been abandoned.

On the other hand, she had been well taught by Aldred in the months on the mainland, and her survival skills were well developed. Even without Luke's ability to sense animal presence, she was highly skilled at trapping and foraging so she was confident they would not starve. Having retrieved her knife, she was able to produce a range of weapons both for hunting and for defence. Though it appeared there were few if any predatory animals in the area, and there were no more large appearances by large cats.

Callan was greatly impressed and convinced his luck had indeed changed dramatically. But he was far from passive in contributing to the new partnership. As he had mentioned, he had been the apprentice tanner in Abbas. Once a supply of animal skins appeared as a result of Marsha's successful hunting, he was remarkably adept at curing and working with the materials. With ingenuity born from necessity he developed tools and other implements to produce a whole set of new clothing for Marsha She was, incidentally, quite impressed with his eye for style, and even more grateful for the wonderfully comfortable footwear he produced, not least because the boots she'd worn since Coldharbour were virtually falling apart.

The nearby stream was deep enough to bathe in and and Callan even managed to combine compounds from local rocks to convert the animal fats into a crude but effective soap. Marsha had not been this clean since the escape from home and delighted in feeling comfortable and well dressed.

With the improvement in diet, Callan himself began to look rather healthier, and the two companions gradually expanded their horizons, exploring the locality and mentally mapping out its features, including the best places for hunting or foraging. Indeed, in one place where the river broadened out, Marsha was able to wade out and patiently wait until a big fat river fish passed by, settled in her hands and suddenly found itself grabbed and flung ashore towards the incredulous Callan.

"You are an absolute marvel!" he shouted in admiration. "However, did you learn to do that? I didn't even know fish were edible!"

"You wait until I roast this in leaves, basted in those tasty herbs I found the other day, Callan. You won't believe anything could taste so good."

Over supper, Callan was forced to agree that it was possibly the best meal he had ever eaten. And looking at Marsha in that misty twilight, for the first time in his life he felt himself surprisingly attracted to someone other than Portha, the woman who had always filled his every romantic thought.

"Tell me about the place you come from and maybe how you got to be here," he asked. "You've been here some time now and you always find a way to avoid telling me about it and where it is?"

"I suppose that's comes from what Aldred explained about our community being a sort of extreme Forgetter one, where secrecy, fear of discovery and mistrust of strangers are so inbuilt that we are hugely reluctant to share anything about our home. But you hardly seem a stranger any more, and I suppose if I don't tell you how to find Coldharbour, it won't hurt."

So as they relaxed after a feast of fish, tubers and wild mushrooms, Marsha told much about the way she and the Coldharbour folk lived, of fishing, farming and Feeling, and of being cut off from the rest of the world - a world they inherently feared and mistrusted. It was too late that night to tell the whole story of the coming of Aldred and how he had turned hers and Luke's lives upside down. But there were more nights when they settled down in the now much more comfortable cave that was, strangely feeling more like a home than any Marsha had lived in.

Perhaps it was just the stability that was a welcome change, after so many months of uncertainly, of moving on and learning new things, and it was so wonderful to benefit from all the lessons she had learnt from Aldred. So in further evenings Marsha told more of their story. However, she was always careful to ensure she didn't give away the location of her childhood home, even though she knew poor Callan had not the slightest sea-going ability (leave alone the Feeling needed to enter in the first place) and bore not the tiniest risk to the folk upon whom she had, in any case, turned her back.

The strange thing that arose quite early in the tale was the fact, obvious, once she got to think about it that Callan knew Aldred, since he had encountered him in Abbas. He was able to fill in some more details about Aldred's past that he had never shared with Luke and her. How he had arrived with his wife and their child, Sharla, whose Mage abilities he had identified and wanted to hide from the Empire.

Much of this she knew, as this was clearly the young girl he'd been reluctant to hand over to the Emperors (though the fact that she was his daughter had some how been missed from Aldred's tale!) However, she now learnt that, some months down the line, Dorcas had needed to find out what was happening back in the centre of things and Aldred had been persuaded to look into it.

Callan explained that the Abbas community was essentially a group of renegades who had fallen out with Imperial rule for a variety of reasons. They weren't in essence an opposition or a rebellion against it, but their set-up would be seen as antithetical to the ruling powers and, if discovered, they would be persecuted and probably killed. Callan's father, for instance, had objected when his sister's magery had been identified and the child ripped from her family home. It wasn't a major rebellion, but he'd realised his life was in danger as a result and had fled north with his wife and son. He'd stumbled across some scouts from Abbas who, when they heard his story and realised a tanner would be a useful addition to their group, introduced him to it.

There was considerable concern that, whereas for a long time, Abbas had been pretty much left alone by the Empire, Camrin's Corps were now seeking to widen their sphere of operations. Knowing that the Abbas community was doing nothing to increase its threat to the Empire, Dorcas wanted to know the reason for this change in policy?

Aldred had left to investigate, and that was the last they'd seen of him, a mystery that at last Marsha was able to solve.

"He told us that unfortunately, in some remote coastal village, he was recognised by someone who reported him to the authorities. He managed to escape by stealing a small fishing boat; the very one in fact that he was sailing in what he stumbled across Luke's illicit fishing trip," she told him.

"Strange how the wheels of fate turn," mused Callan.

"Whatever does that mean?" asked Marsha? "What are 'Wheels of Fate?'"

"Not a clue!" he laughed. "Just an expression, I suppose. I'm told we often use expressions from past ages but their meanings are lost in time. Maybe they were some sort of mersheen from the ages of gineering?"

"These mersheens sound fascinating, Callan. Have people found out any more?" she asked.

"Not much, from what I hear. Though they have discovered some books and some of them have pictures of mersheens, they think."

"Books? What are books?" she asked again.

"Not really sure, Marsha, as I've never seen one. But I understand the ancients had some way of recording their language on sheets of a material that was soft and white, with markings in black. It doesn't need teck to interpret it, but you need to know what the markings mean. Some of our people were working on that, but it was all very secret and I don't know how far they'd got."

"Those ancients must've been very clever and advanced," said Marsha, enthralled.

"Not advanced enough to stop them blowing themselves up!" retorted Callan.

***

Another night, their conversation looked more to the future than the past.

Marsha broached the subject of what they should do next? They were managing quite well and had created a safe and fairly comfortable base, but she felt there was no particular purpose to staying where they were. Now that Callan was stronger and healthier, she suggested they might explore a bit farther afield to see if she might make contact with the folk from Abbas, and possibly reunite with Aldred and Luke?

Initially Callan was extremely reluctant even to consider such a move, but over time, events made him more open to it. Several times they spotted evidence of groups of men camped near the borders of the wood where they were based. Though there was no certainty that these were Camrin's Corps, nor had any encroached into the woods themselves, Callan's feeling of vulnerability began to increase.

Marsha worked on the doubt this engendered and was finally able to persuade him that possibly he could guide her to find his own community, even if he didn't initially join her when she met them. Maybe, she reasoned, she could engage Aldred - who Callan had indicated had some influence in the community - to listen to the evidence, establish the facts and, belatedly clear Callan's name?

Over time, Callan began to see that staying where they were was not a long-term option, especially as winter set in, with foraging and hunting already getting harder. Before he had finally agreed, however, something occurred which was strange and unsettling to them both.

One evening, after another successful find of some particularly delicious plants that only erupted from the ground during the Autumn. Marsha had cooked them with some hare that had been hung to perfection, augmented by some roasted cob nuts. The whole lot was followed by apples, baked slowly in the outer parts of the fire whilst the main meal was cooking. Marsha had remarked earlier that the aromas were so delicious and powerful that she was a bit worried in case any passers by smelt them.

Suddenly, Callan looked very concerned and said he could hear voices.

"Not possible," suggested Marsha, "because if they were close enough for us to hear talking, our trip sets would have warned us."

Marsha had long ago initiated the practice, taught her by Aldred, of arranging sets of ingeniously arranged twigs that were impossible to pass by without warning the pair of approaching animals or people.

"I can hear them!" he insisted. "Listen!'

However, instead of simply listening, Marsha found herself concentrating so hard, a bit like Feeling, while looking at Callan. Suddenly, she found herself, in a strange way, hearing voices too!.

It was difficult to describe but somehow she was melding her concentration into Callan's thoughts and adding into his own levels of focus. At the same time not only did she hear what he heard, but he found himself hearing the 'voices' even louder. Yet somehow they didn't seem any closer and were distinctly garbled. Very different from a conversation.

"It's almost like we're reading thoughts," he remarked, somewhat perplexed.

"That's it!" gasped Marsha. "You must be some sort of Mage who can read thoughts!" she exclaimed. But as she spoke, the 'volume' of the thoughts dropped from Callan, and Marsha herself could no longer 'hear' them.

"Concentrate again," he suggested, as they realised this was happening. Sure enough when she re-focussed her mind, she once again made a connection with his magery as together they sought to understand the thoughts being transmitted.

With practice they were able to improve their working together focusing their minds simultaneously on the thoughts they seemed to be tracking. It was a struggle to make out or interpret these thoughts, which seemed to be incoherent and jump all over the place.

There was, however a sense of caution and fear. Somehow they ascertained that whoever these thoughts belonged, the person was some fair distance away. That meant, of course, they had not tripped the warning traps and, as the mind moved away, the thoughts and feelings faded until there was nothing much beyond a gentle muffled 'noise.'

Relaxing and letting go, the two companions felt a strange mixture of released tension, weariness and elation.

"That was amazing!" said Marsha, eventually.

"And strange, too! Imagine me, Callan, with magery within me! But what sort of magery was it, I wonder?"

Marsha thought for a while, until, remembering the session she had overheard with Aldred, she said, "It sounds like you are a Pather - one of those rare Mages who can read minds. Some are said to be able to affect thoughts and influence people to make them do things ... or that might be Melding? Have you never noticed your gift before?"

"No, never. Not at all. I was just thinking then, and my mind was wondering, and there were the noises. Strange, because you were right next to me and I couldn't hear your thoughts at all. But somehow became aware of those others. By the way, what were you doing? How did you focus and strengthen what I was doing? Is that some sort of magery too?"

"I suppose so," said Marsha slowly. "Aldred said he could sense magery within me but it was somehow different, and he couldn't work out what it was, apart for my ability with Feeling that is. He wondered if living at Coldharbour in our closed society had produced new mageries. He'd said that Luke's gifts were different and new, too Did I tell you about the time he made us all Unseen?"

"Unseen? Whatever does that mean?"

"So that we couldn't be seen or detected?"

"Sort of invisible? He could disappear?"

"Well, yes ... but in some ways it was better than that. It was almost as if the whole group of us just weren't there."

And Marsha told more of that first incident behind the rock and how subsequently Aldred had taught Luke to concentrate and vary his approach, in order to strengthen his power and control it and how he had discovered Marsha's gift of accentuating Luke's abilities.

She suggested that they too might wish to collaborate this with their new-found gifts, but, sadly they would have to do so without Aldred's tutoring skills.

"But you think if we found Aldred, the process could be easier, maybe?" asked Callan.

"Well, yes of course. He's an experienced Seeker who has spent his life identifying and training new Mages, even if in recent times his principal role has been to betray the most powerful ones, to be dealt with by Camrin and Magrat. He found that really hard and he's committed to opposing that pair now but, yes, he would be really useful to our quest to explore your gifts. I have to say again that I'm missing both his presence and his wisdom. I don't think we can go on living here much longer without needing more than I can offer. It could be a hard winter, and I'm not sure I've got the experience to keep us going."

For the first time in such conversations, Callan didn't answer with a "Yes ... but ..." Rather it was, "I suppose so. And I suppose if I could hone my Pather skills to be more aware of who was near me, I could risk getting close to the Abbas folk, wherever they are, without the risk of being discovered?"

"Even better, Callan: you might possibly be able to use your skills to track down where they are actually living now!"

"Maybe? Yes, that's possible. It's all so strange and unexpected! But I do think it helps me risk leaving this place. On one condition: that we set up some stores here, so that if I have to flee I can get back here, and have something to keep me going for a while. Though to be honest, having had company these weeks I'm not sure I want to be alone again. I don't think I could stand it. You've made such a difference. Before you came I was starving and desperate and it's not just the fact that you have such brilliant survival skills; it's just been so wonderful to have someone to share my time with."

"Well thank you, kind sir! And while we're giving thanks, can I say you've been a perfect gentleman to share a cave with! Not to mention that it's wonderful to wear clothes that fit and don't stink! I think I've learnt a great deal from you and enjoyed your company too. However, I do think the time has come to move on, and we need more than we can get here on our own.

"We need the others. I also, really, really do think, if Dorcas is as wise a leader as you say, Aldred should be able to persuaded her that you are not the rapist they say you are. You will have a witness that you have shared a cave with a woman for months, and never been anything but perfectly respectful!"

"I do hope you're not insulted by my lack of approach? It's just, my heart belongs to Portha and, lovely and attractive as you are, I sort of still hope that one day ...?"

"Not insulted at all, Callan, and indeed, rather flattered. Nobody's ever called me attractive before!"

"Not even your friend Luke?"

"No, not yet, though I get the impression he thinks it, maybe."

"Is that why you helped rescue him? Because you thought he was attractive too?"

She laughed, a little awkwardly. "No, I don't think so. I think we have a lot in common, not least a desire to develop our magery gifts, but I think my greatest motivation was to do something to make life in Coldharbour better. Luke suggested it was reaching a crisis and I felt there might be something out here in the Outland that we could take back. It was one of his more mature thoughts, and, to be honest he'll need to do a bit more growing up before I could think about getting together with him"

Callan nodded in understanding as Marsha said, "So, yes, let's stock up. We've already got quite a lot of dried meat, and I know where there are some decent stocks of tubers, and mushrooms that are nearly ready to harvest. They will keep well, and we could gather them in advance to leave as a store in case you need to retreat here.

"I've also got supplies of a root that tastes like nothing worth eating but is full of energy, and can keep us going on our travels. With all the wonderful leather bags you've made, I think we could pack them up and carry enough for a week or more without wearing ourselves out. We can supplement our rations with what we hunt on the way, so that gives us a fortnight or more to explore. Do you think they'll have moved farther than that?"

"No, I don't think so. I got the impression they had a pretty good idea where they were moving to. There was a rumour that there was already a retreat area up in the mountains where Camrin's Corps never dared go. I think if we went that way, we should find them pretty soon. And, apart from the open area where you got separated from your friends, most of it has good cover. We should be safe. So, when do you think we might be leaving?"

Marsha couldn't quite believe she was hearing the question or how suddenly Callan's mind had changed. Funny, looking back, how Luke's decisions had resulted from the suggestion that he, likewise had magery gifts! It has also been the suggestion that Marsha, too, had magery within her makeup which had helped her decide to initiate the great escape from Coldharbour. Then again, look at all the trouble that had caused!

Nevertheless the logjam had been broken. "I suppose a few days is all we'll need, if that's ok with you?" she suggested.

"Sounds good to me. Let's get some sleep, now, eh?"

"We have a plan, my friend," said Marsha, relieved. Under her breath she added, "Let's hope it's a good plan. We're going to need one!"

Part 4 - Aldred

16 HOPE

Aldred set off with all the speed he could muster but was hampered by several issues. Firstly, in his desperation to get out of the spider run he had climbed out its southern side, and needed to travel quite some way to find a place where he could traverse it. In his youth he might have taken a long run and attempted to jump over it, but in his current weariness he knew that wasn't possible.

His state of tiredness after a long day, his wounds and scratches from battles with the large cats, not to mention the mental energy expended in order to persuade the stubborn teenager, was his second issue. It meant he really was terribly weary and, hurry as best he could, he was taking longer than he would wish. He kept looking up at the sun, approaching the horizon far too quickly, and cursing under his breath.

Eventually he encountered a large fallen tree that had fallen across the spiders' run and, pausing only long enough to note that this had clearly been deliberately chopped down to provide such passage, he crossed over and headed for the outcrop that he knew led to the hidden community on the edges of the mountain range.

He had expected that outlying lookouts would have hailed him long before he arrived at the village but, with dusk approaching rapidly, he finally rounded the corner of a winding, convoluted and cunningly concealed path to enter Abbas.

A day before he had anticipated approaching with triumph and expectation in his heart, looking forward to meeting old friends and introducing his new companions to them. Today, instead, his entrance was one full of woe, exhaustion and, to his horror, desperate disappointment!

The place was empty and, by the look of it, had been abandoned for some time.

Aldred fell to his knees in desolation. He'd promised to do his best and to bring aid to his young charge, a teenager he had enticed to leave home on what now appeared to be a fool's errand to challenge a mighty Empire. He dropped his head into his hands, asking himself, dejectedly, how he could have been so idiotic to think he could even try?

What had Marsha, that kind, clever, able girl called him? Oh yes: 'idealistic.'

Yeah, she'd got that right, hadn't she, as she had so many things right before (apart perhaps for falling for his dreams and idealism?) That lovely young person was - where? The leftovers of a big cat's meal, just as her friend was probably about to become one for a giant spider? What had he done to them? What had they done to deserve the fates he had led them to, he cried out?

But as he knelt there in despair, he became aware that the daylight was slipping away and, just possibly, if he could find something to pull Luke out, and if he could get back to him in time, there might be a way of delivering on his promises. He'd been through trials before, and sitting on the ground hadn't gotten him through them!

Desperately he searched though the empty village, disappointed again and again at how efficiently the folk had cleared out everything of value. Until, that is, he came across the blacksmith's workshop. "Trust that sloppy git to leave things!" he said to himself as he espied a large metal bar and, delightfully, a decent length of rope.

Reenergised with a weapon and the possibility of rescuing Luke, Aldred set off back the way he had come. It was getting darker and darker, and increasingly hard to find his route. Fortunately the ditch-crossing tree was distinctive in the dark and, despite his increasing tiredness, he was able to cross it and retrace his steps to the place where he had left Luke to his fate.

"Luke! Luke!" he called but received no reply.

"Luke!" he called again and again.

But nothing!

For the second time in a day Aldred dropped to the ground, and this time he wept uncontrollably. Then, with the combination of exhaustion and despair at the immensity of his failure too much for mind and body, he passed out and fell into a deep, deep sleep.

***

In the morning he awoke rested but, not surprisingly, his mood remained unchanged. He was stiff, cold and desperately alone. He had become used in the past to being on his own but now, after a period of companionship and growing relationship with his … what? Yes, his friends, his comrades, his team, his family almost: he was bereft. To make it worse, he had been looking forward to reunion with his other family, yet they, too, were gone.

He was tempted to sit there and let his life slip away, as all his hopes had already done.

Yet hope, sometimes, glimmers on, almost unseen, like a tiny candle light flickering in the darkness.

As he sat there hunched up and distraught, he noticed a small tree nearby and a thought entered his mind. If Luke had met his end down below in the spider run, wouldn't there be evidence?

Tying his rope to nearby tree, he lowered himself down into the ditch-like structure and looked around. Yes, there were the bloodstains where Luke had lain as they had argued about trust. And over there were fresh marks - deep gouges in the side of the run. Signs of a struggle maybe, he thought? Luke had, after all, been armed with his spear. Possibly creature and human had battled; maybe even, Luke had overcome it?

With that hopeful thought flickering slightly more strongly, Aldred set off along the run a bit. Just to see.

Some three hundred or so strides around the corner his heart leapt a little as, before his eyes there lay a huge, collapsed and very dead spider. Investigation left him in no doubt that Luke had indeed vanquished it, for there, sticking out of it was his spear, deeply embedded in the creature's head parts.

But where was Luke? There was no evidence of a human body, no blood: nothing apart from the spear. Why, if Luke had overcome the beast, had he not reclaimed that, not least as he had suggested the day before, he would need it as a walking support?

Where was Luke? Why wasn't he here? And how had he gotten out of the deep ditch without aid, when it had taken every effort of Aldred and Luke together?

With too many questions and no answers forthcoming, Aldred nevertheless found himself encouraged. It seemed that somehow, possibly, Luke had escaped and was alive. And if so, it was surely incumbent on Aldred to stay alive himself and endeavour to find him again?

So, with hope burning just a little brighter within him, Aldred walked back to his rope, clambered up out of the dread-filled ditch and decided, for now to return to the abandoned village of Abbas.

17 ALONE

Back in survival mode, though, before wearily returning to the empty settlement that had once been his home, Aldred made a brief diversion. Having managed now for nearly two days solely on water from streams, he went back first to the scene of the cat attack, to retrieve the packs they had abandoned in their rush to find Marsha. There he was mightily relieved to find them mostly intact, despite the local wildlife having made some attempts to raid their contents. At least he would have some food for a week or so, augmented no doubt by some foraging. It gave him some breathing space, anyway.

Suitably refreshed by a quick meal (he was worried there might be more wild cats and the locality was very open) he set off back to Abbas, where once again he felt hugely lonely. He had not only become used to company, he had developed a way of planning in his head and then sharing and discussing it with the other two. Despite previous years of lone-working, he now found he so greatly missed the second stage, that every time he started to plan, he found his mind meandering all over the place and failing to come up with any sort of strategy.

Cursing this inability, he decided on an interim policy of allowing himself to recover physically from the trials of the last few days. "The future can take care of itself." he thought to himself. "For now, I need to focus on the here and now!"

So he did, settling back into his former lodging where Mahanda, Sharla and he had stayed, rummaging around all the other buildings in the settlement for anything useful that had been left behind. There was precious little, apart from a pair of stout, well-fitting boots and, delightfully, some items of clothing, which were a little large but at least, clean! He also found a large knife plus a bow and arrows, which would make hunting just that bit easier now that he lacked the input from super-hunter Luke!

Fresh meat was available, he discovered, when he stumbled upon a number of hens who had avoided being rounded up. Tempting them back to the cottage with some crumbs and seeds, he was able to pen them in once again. After a period without company, however, he couldn't quite persuade himself to butcher them. His reluctance was rewarded, since caring for them gave him structure to to his day, which was healing in itself. Even better, within a week, they blessed him further, with fresh eggs!

***

As he had hoped, this period of several weeks enabled him to regain his equilibrium and his mental acuity began to improve. Armed with his bow, he quickly redeveloped his shooting skills and downed several birds as they flew by the settlement. Tough as the meat was to chew, at least it augmented his dried supplies and was welcome and healing too, enabling him to start thinking and planning for the future once more.

It also accentuated his ability to see things that he hadn't noticed before. Thus, one evening as he settled down in the crudely built habitation, he began musing about how once upon a time, this rough and roughly built structure had felt like a warm and comfortable home. Having lectured Luke so recently on trust, he was suddenly rather aware how he had kept back details about his own personal circumstances - and the full details and reasons why he had fled from the Empire.

Musing on this, he knelt down to set the fire and noticed suddenly that one of the stones beside the hearth was different from the rest. Strangely, it seemed to lack any mortar and was less soot-stained than the others surrounding the fireplace.

"That's odd!" he said out loud. "I know I set that myself properly. Why would anyone...? And then thought again. "That's not strange, that's deliberate! Mahanda, you clever old thing, you! I'll bet ..." he said, and began to wiggle the large stone. Sure enough, it was slightly loose and, after much effort and leverage with the knife and, then the metal bar he'd retrieved from the blacksmith's, he succeeded in pulling the stone out of the wall.

There, at the back of the space was a bag of gold coins and a piece of parchment, carefully folded and with a large M and an X upon it. "Ah, Mahanda!" he said as he reached in and pulled it out.

The parchment was slightly damp and rather mildewed, and in the poor light of the fading day he could not read what it said. He lit the fire but, set up as usual to be inconspicuous, it did not produce much light. His protective instincts weren't going to be overridden even in these exciting circumstances, so, patiently he decided to wait until morning to read it properly.

That night he settled into a delightful reverie as he realised his beloved partner had believed he would return and wanted to ensure that he would know where she and the renegades had moved on to. "Clever, clever, wonderful old thing," he thought again as he slipped off to sleep in front of the fire.

***

Aldred awoke early, refreshed and excited. The dawn light was streaming in so he spread out the parchment and tried to decipher its meaning. He was mighty glad he hadn't attempted to read it the night before as, being slightly damp, its marks were easily smudged and could have made it unreadable. After a night open and partially dried, he could at least begin to read its scrawls and symbols. Mahanda presumably believed he would understand her coded message, though it would be incomprehensible to anyone else.

There was a mountain above a house-shape, a line of dots, first eastwards and later further northwards, and then another house next to several trees. He wondered if the houses represented where he was now - Abbas, at the foot of mountains - and then, maybe, Mahanda's current position, somewhere in a forest? If so, however, there was not sufficient detail for him to find it!

There was, though, also an image that looked like a well-head, including rope and bucket, but it lay on its side.

He scratched his head in deep incomprehension. The best Aldred could conclude was that his beloved thought he was cleverer than he actually was!

Having started off once again with his hopes building up, Aldred was now feeling deeply frustrated. However, something else attracted his attention.

In all this time in Abbas, there had been no noise, apart from the wind and his chickens. He suddenly became aware, though, of distant footsteps and voices. Could some Abbas folk be back and checking their old site, he wondered.

Rushing to the door he looked around the corner of the building to see, to his horror, a group of men led by one with that tell-tale red feather on his cap. They were some way down the hill, near the entrance to the settlement, but he really hadn't much time to dash back inside, gather his few goods together quickly, and do his best to remove evidence of recent occupation.

As silently as he could he slipped back out of the house and crept uphill, always attempting to keep buildings between him and any chance the Corps might have of seeing him as he fled. It appeared that they were currently resting, having discovered the settlement was uninhabited. But they would no doubt start searching around soon and would find a dwelling that had obviously been lived in recently, with a warm hearth amongst other giveaways, whereupon they would certainly give chase.

Reassuring himself that at least he knew the layout, and there were two escape routes out, Aldred crept further upwards to the top of the settlement. However, this left him in a bit of a quandary. The nearest exit was well hidden, and he would be near it quite soon, but had the disadvantage of being on the west side of the village. Using it would give him a hard journey westwards, through narrow and dangerous mountain paths and, ultimately, leave him miles away from the route he wished to take to the new Abbas location. The farther, more northerly escape path would quickly lead him eastwards and in the preferred direction, but only if he had time to get to it without being seen.

The decision, though, was made for him as he, heard movement below him in the settlement, as the troops ended their brief rest and began to search around. Ducking down behind a row of cottages he crawled along below a row of bushes leading to a large but unremarkable rock beside a holly bush. Squeezing carefully between the two (very carefully since the leaves were sharp), he slipped out of Abbas, aware that it was extremely unlikely that the Corps would voluntarily do likewise.

As he did so, he heard a raised voice, signalling that his recent presence had been discovered and confirming his wise choice of the earlier escape route. Even though it would mean a significantly longer and harder journey, at least he had a chance now of getting away without capture. As quietly as he could, he crept gently away, feeling very slightly smug at how well that morning had gone, all things considered.

Quick thinking, organised and calm! It was how he had survived for some years, he thought to himself. "Thank goodness I found the note last night." he said, confidently, patting his pocket holding the note with the coded directions to New Abbas.

Except it wasn't there!

Somehow, he realised with a sinking heart, in his escape he had dropped it. Would the Imperial Corps find it? If they did, would they realise its significance? Surely if so, they wouldn't be able to interpret its coded message, he reasoned? After all, he was struggling to understand it himself. But if they could: had he just betrayed his friends and loved ones' location through an act of sheer carelessness?

All smugness had suddenly evaporated as he returned to what was becoming a far too familiar pose: a hunched up, despondent Aldred with face in hands. What had he done? What had he done?

18 RESOLUTION

Aldred, though, hadn't survived this long by giving in to despair and, after what seemed like hours (but was probably only 30 minutes or so) rocking himself back and forth, his rational brain began to start reasserting itself over his emotional devastation. His error needn't be catastrophic though potentially it had made finding the Abbas community more urgent.

Carefully and as quietly as possible, he made his way along the narrow pathway that led away from Abbas. It was longer than he had remembered but he supposed the last time he had been this way he had been in a light mood, enjoying the company of his friends as they taught him the escape route he hoped he'd never need to take. He had also been younger and fitter, he reminded himself!

How different it was when he so sorely missed his comrades and worried about how they were - if indeed they were even alive? He doubted if Marsha had made it, since the last time he had seen her, she was being pursued by a ferocious cat. Even if Luke had escaped, as he seemed to have done from the spiders' run, he wondered if he, too had any realistic chance of getting very far and surviving for very long with what might have been a broken leg?

He ruminated further: had it been wise or indeed fair to have roped in these two young folk into his adventures, even if they had seemingly joined him voluntarily? They were idealistic and innocent, ambitious even, and he wondered if he had possibly manipulated them unfairly?

But then he began to think more warmly of their time together. The teamwork they had developed as they had taken so well to the lessons in survival - blossomed even - exhibiting surprising skills and abilities that complemented each other. Skills indeed that at this moment he missed almost as much as he missed their company.

Nevertheless, he was where he was and, hard as it was to be on his own, he had to recognise that he had survived alone before and he could do so again.

He travelled on for a few days, focusing on finding water, food and shelter. Nights spent in caves were markedly more comfortable, and indeed safer, than sleeping out in the open air with nobody to share periods of watch, but he carried on travelling and wondering. The weather was getting colder as winter set in, and he didn't reckon he could survive indefinitely.

Eventually he travelled further than before but recalled that he'd been told that this route away from Abbas took him over a river. When he got there, it was rather deeper than he had expected and he had to half swim, half wade through it. Still soaked through, he then encountered a long, deep canyon He had been expecting this but, frustratingly, it had become blocked by a hefty rockfall. Aldred's attempt to climb over it took nearly an hour via several routes over the unstable pile. When he finally ended up on the other side of the barrier, he was absolutely exhausted, bruised and distinctly demoralised.

He realised he could not continue like this and would need to find a village to get some supplies and perhaps give himself a further period of recuperation before he set off for the Abbas community. Fortunately, the 'escape route' as he thought of it, was coming to an end as he entered a wooded area and could turn first southwards and then eastwards, in the general direction where he believed the Abbas community to be. Woods and forest, as he had always said, provided cover but it could be difficult to be sure you were traveling in the desired direction.

Nevertheless, his skills were well honed, his progress steady and, as he had taught the young pair, there was usually food to scavenge in woodland, even if he had also to be aware of the dangers of wildlife that would happily make a meal of him!

✻✻✻

Remembering a village to the south of Abbas, Aldred travelled as directly as he could that way. He knew some of the folks there for it had been the last place he had stayed before discovering Abbas. He'd decided it was safer to live amongst the renegades rather than constantly being on guard in Offwell, living in constant fear of a Seeker visit to the village. His navigating skills were not quite as good as he had believed but he eventually noted some landmarks which struck a chord and he carefully approached the village, pleased that there didn't appear to be any signs of Imperial Corps in the locality.

The night before he arrived, he set a trap in the hope of catching some rabbits which would provide him a cover story as a trapper and trader. Woken up by sounds of a huge struggle, he was delighted to find he had successfully trapped a decent sized deer instead. He dispatched it, and felt rather pleased with himself, only to wish yet again that Luke was there, so that he could boast of his achievement!

In the morning, with his prize on his back, Aldred approached the village of Offwell, feeling more positive than he had for a while. The villagers, however, were much changed from the welcoming and hospitable folk he had encountered in the past. They treated him with great suspicion, even if they did seem to welcome the possibility of some fresh game to augment their own provisions.

The general consensus was that they should simply take the game off him and kick him out. However, in the midst of these discussions, a middle-aged woman arrived and pushed her way through the rowdy crowd.

"Well blow me down, it's Alpert, isn't it?" she asked.

Aldred nodded sheepishly, remembering the name he had assumed whilst staying there previously.

"Well come on, everybody! Surely you remember good old Alpert? With Manda and Shandi? Lovely family, and harmless? And a great hunter too if I remember rightly. We could do with a bit of extra food, couldn't we, friends? He never caused us any problems - and look at him, he's not only lost his wife and daughter it looks like he's lost a load of weight, too? Surely we can't toss an old friend out? We live in difficult times - but have we really lost all our hospitality and kindness?" she asked looking around, daring anyone to contradict her.

When one voice said uncertainly, "Yeah, but where will he stay, Ellen?" the woman laughed and said that he was so small these days, he could easily fit in her cottage and she was sure her husband wouldn't mind!

Ellen was clearly a force to be reckoned with and, after little further discussion, Aldred was mightily relieved that the Elders agreed, especially as they also traded some food for some of his venison.

That evening in Ellen's cottage, she was very keen to hear of his adventures since last he had visited. He shared his usual cover story of travelling and struggling to settle down anywhere. Usually he was rather pleased with his tale-spinning, which was credible and, even more important, incredibly boring, so his listeners always got fed up long before he got to the end! However, he was somewhat worried that Ellen kept returning to the fact that he was no longer travelling with Mahanda and she never looked completely convinced by his responses.

He was, though, able to interrogate Ellen in turn to see what had happened in this part of Southfleet in the months since he had been absent. Her tales explained the suspiciousness of the Offwell folk compared with their past welcome. Apparently groups of Imperial Corps, who had previously only appeared every other year, often with a Seeker wanting to track down Mages, were now visiting more and more frequently. When they did, they demanded food and lodging, kicking folk out of their cottages for the duration of their visits and taking any supplies they could lay their hands on when they left.

The villagers, who had previously lived reasonably comfortably, were finding it harder and harder to survive, living in an atmosphere of fear. In past years, their worries had been of raiders from Ruark in the north. These days, they instead lived in dread of a visit from their own Empire's forces, and had taken to hiding spare supplies in store houses outside of the village, but they were terrified that if these were found by the Corps, they would be punished.

She did say that some of the more junior soldiers were a bit more friendly, looked uncomfortable and even apologised for their actions sometimes. However, they couldn't disobey the orders of their superiors and the situation was getting more and more desperate.

As they talked, Aldred became aware of an increasingly delicious smell emanating from Ellen's oven He was thrilled beyond words when she eventually took out a loaf of freshly-baked bread for their lunch.

Bread!

He'd forgotten the basic and fundamental wonderfulness of freshly baked bread, which he hadn't eaten since Coldharbour. As they sat and talked and reminisced, whilst reflecting on the awful current situation, he bit into the gorgeously tasty bread and, just for a moment, life felt hopeful again.

Ellen's husband came home, and confirmed that he was happy for Aldred to stay with them for a while, as long as he could make a contribution to the household's village share of produce. Aldred suggested that his trapping skills (already confirmed by his arrival with a deer) might be helpful, augmenting the meat from domesticated animals, whose numbers had been reduced by the frequent raids from the Imperial Corps.

It seemed a sensible plan. Aldred was exhausted and needed time once again to recuperate and recharge himself, not to mention a safe and secure base to get through the winter. It was less likely that the Corps would visit during these colder months, so it ought to be safer too, he reasoned. Admittedly, he was worried that the Corps members back in Abbas might have deciphered Mahanda's note, but the more time passed, the less this bothered him. He did, after all, need to survive himself and the escape from Abbas had left him weakened and exhausted. He just had to hope that if they had discovered it, then they would be as dense as him deciphering its coded clues!

Over time the villagers' antagonism and suspicion lessened, especially as his regular contributions of game were greatly welcomed. His luck with trapping and hunting continued for some weeks, and he was beginning to feel reasonably settled and very much stronger. The weather, though, was definitely getting worse as well as considerably colder and the thought of travelling onwards became both less attractive and somehow less and and less urgent.

Nevertheless, Aldred set up a hidden camp in the woods with all his possessions, such as they were, stored there. If the Corps should visit the village, he would be able to slip away, leaving no evidence in Ellen's cottage of their lodger and, if necessary, he could flee without having to pack.

It was while visiting his hideout one evening, to return his hunting equipment, that he was suddenly struck as, unusually, he spoke his thoughts out loud. "I suspect the good folks of Offwell will be a bit disappointed by three rabbits and a brace of pheasants. I hope I'm a bit luckier tomorrow! It's a bit off ... but ... ah well!"

He stood still as if winded as he said it and then, laughed out loud.

"Offwell? Off ... well? Oh, of course!" he exclaimed. "But how?"

What had hit him was the sudden realisation that he had now been some weeks in the very place Mahanda had been referring to in her coded note. Hadn't there been an image of a well-head, but, obscurely, lying on its side? Could that possibly be an 'off well'?

What, then, had she meant by that? Was she suggesting there was another clue here in this village of Offwell - a place where they had lived for some time, maybe? And if so, where would it be?

Still pondering this, he headed back with his prizes. His distraction, though, almost led to a fatal mistake as he approached the village far too openly and not looking ahead for dangers. Once again, however, he was fortunate in meeting Ellen as he was about to leave the cover of the trees.

"Stop Aldred! Get back behind the trees!" she hissed at him

He immediately jumped back, just before a member of the Corps only yards away looked up and shouted at Ellen, "You there! Get back to the village. Now!"

"Yes sir, I will, I was just collecting these field mushrooms to bring back! I'm coming, sir!" Then, with a lowered voice she whispered to Aldred, "Hide in the woods for a few days before coming back to Offwell. See you after that!"

"Thanks!" he whispered back, and stayed stock still as she and the member of the Corps headed downhill and gradually out of sight.

Cursing his stupidity, he began to believe that he was losing his survival instincts. How could he have been so daft as to waltz out of cover without even looking first? How could he have allowed himself to be so distracted?

But later, after he had returned to his hideout camp, deeper in the woods, another thought flashed into his mind. "How come she hissed 'Aldred' to me and not 'Alpert'?" he suddenly thought. "This place is more and more worrying! I don't think I can stay much longer ... not least because I'm beginning to talk to myself!"

***

Three days later, having periodically checked from a distance and seen the Corps heading off southwards, he surreptitiously slipped back into the village, where a very weary-looking Ellen and her husband met them with resigned expressions.

"That was a close thing, Aldred! Just lucky I was collecting those mushrooms, otherwise they'd've had you!"

"Indeed," he replied, "and many thanks for your timely warning. But how come you're suddenly calling me by my real name? What's going on?"

"Well, my friend," Ellen said wryly, "you're not the only one who can do subterfuge, you know!"

"You what? I mean …?" he started to say, but Ellen was in no mood to be interrupted.

"Just sit down at the table and have a meal, Aldred. I'm afraid it's going to be your last here for a while. And while you're eating, I have a story for you."

As he meekly complied, she started her tale.

"About a year ago, Mahanda (or Manda as I had previously known her) and a group of Abbas folks came to visit us here in Offwell. She told me much more than she had previously shared about your role and background and why you were a wanted man in the Empire."

"She should never have done that, Ellen," said an exasperated Aldred, "It put you in danger as well as us. Our cover story was supposed to protect you and …"

"I know. I know, but it was necessary. Please, just listen and I will explain. And eat - you will need a full stomach after what I've told you!

"So, Mahanda said that she had grown to trust us two and needed to extend that trust by sharing the truth. She had learnt that the Abbas folk, fearful of discovery had implemented a plan to build an alternative village further in the forests to the northeast of here. A bit like your hideout camp in our woods. They were worried that the Corps were scouting so close and so frequently that they would inevitably stumble across Abbas. Since so many of the Abbas folk are renegades and wanted by the authorities, such a visit would be even more catastrophic than it is when they visit here.

"Mahanda, though, was worried that if they had to move to a new Abbas you would return to the old one and find them gone and …"

"That's exactly what happened, Ellen."

"We guessed as much, which only goes to show how clever your Mahanda is! She said she planned to leave a coded message for you in your cottage to come here. Then we could direct you to their location."

"So all these weeks you've known exactly why I was here, and you never gave me her message? It's taken me until now to work out that she wanted me to come here and you've not done a thing to help me understand it and …"

"Yes, Aldred, I'm sorry about that, but you have to understand we were worried about your health. You looked so haggard that, frankly, we decided you wouldn't survive the journey to the new Abbas. You needed to get stronger and …"

Aldred was absolutely furious at this news. "Don't you think I should've made that decision myself?" he almost shouted.

"Don't you raise your voice!" said Ellen imperiously. "We made a judgement based upon our concern for you. Knowing you, we believed you would probably have insisted on leaving anyway. And we couldn't risk that!"

Aldred laughed, remembering the subterfuge he had used to fool Luke, and suddenly felt angry no more. "And when, exactly, were you going to get around to telling me the truth, I wonder?"

"Soon, honestly, Aldred. In fact we had thought next week, not least as the weather is looking milder, which not only would make your journey better, but make the possibility of Corps visits more likely anyway. But their arrival this week has made it imperative to tell you now … and to tell you that you need to move on as soon as possible, my friend. Not least because as well taking supplies, this group were actually asking about you specifically!"

"What? They were looking for me?"

"Absolutely! Fortunately the Elders stuck to sullenly insisting they had never heard of you, but I'll be honest, I don't think the village folk will be able to resist another interrogation. Your game supplies are good … but not that good!"

They all laughed this time and Aldred thanked Ellen and her husband for their help and support. He admitted that he would almost certainly have ignored their entreaties to stay a while and expressed his gratitude that he was most definitely healthier and stronger now. Ellen gave him the directions he required and he finished his last, delicious meal in their household.

A rough knock on the door, interrupted their tearful farewells as one of the village Elders arrived and encouraged Aldred to leave quickly, one of his scouts had reported the group of Corps appeared to be coming back in their direction.

"It's fine, we've said our goodbyes." Aldred announced, adding, "Though I'm not sure I can say sufficient thank-yous!"

"No need, just go! And good luck!" said Ellen.

Part 5 - Teamwork

19 FOREST ABBAS

The distance to the new Abbas was much greater than Aldred had imagined and was made more difficult because of the large number of Corps patrols in the area, making him take several diversions to give them a wide berth. How he wished he had Luke with him to make them Unseen together en route!

He realised in retrospect, though, that the extra distance made sense. If the Abbas folk were concerned that the Corps were in the locality, it was logical to be a lot farther away from their patrols. On the other hand, this led to two thoughts. Firstly, how long could the community manage by continually running away and hiding? They had managed to survive for some years now on the far extremes of the Empire, where they were unlikely to be bothered or discovered by chance. But now that they had left, in fear of systematic patrols finding them, how long would they be able to avoid a subsequent search party, especially now the Corps were aware of their previous base?

Secondly, they had struggled massively where they had been to be sustainable and to feed the community. Their resources were even fewer than those in Coldharbour, which had left those folk seriously challenged. He greatly feared that a base much farther north and higher yet in the mountains would be even harder to survive in, even if they weren't discovered!

Assuming he reached their new base, Aldred began to realise that he would have to persuade Dorcas and the Elders that they needed to work out a new plan sooner or later. And preferably sooner!

***

Over a fortnight later, tired and finding his initial pace having seriously slowed, Aldred was, nevertheless fairly confident that he was approaching his objective. He stood looking at a large forested area. Mahanda's instructions, relayed to him by Ellen, were to look out for a large rock near a distinctive tree. Failing to find what he was looking for, he did see a rock similar to the rock in question, though it had no particularly identifiable tree nearby.

Perplexed and disappointed, he decided to take a chance and started the arduous climb upwards. His food supplies were beginning to get rather low and recently he had been distinctly unsuccessful with his hunting for game, muttering to himself that he had known his luck would break eventually!

He was, though, grateful for all the foraging skills Marsha had taught him. Tubers, fruits and berries were keeping him alive, but he was hopeful the renegades might treat him to a decent meal on his arrival. Before, that was, he informed them that they might need to leave soon!

Passing by the rock he was surprised to see no evidence of a path through the forest. But maybe this indicated that the Abbas folk were canny enough not to use this as their route inwards, since a well-worn path would be a dead giveaway of their location ahead?

Sure enough his instincts were correct. As he moved inwards into the forested area, he spied occasional flattened bushes and broken branches, indicating regular travel hereabouts. He knew enough to recognise the difference between the routes taken by wild animals and those of humans, though if he were to try to explain it, he would struggle to find the words. He just knew!

He also knew that there would be scouts lying out soon, preparing to look out for intruders and patrols from the Corps. What was more, he remembered some of the whistled sounds that would warn them even earlier of his approach. Repeated whistles that to the uninitiated might sound like birdsong began to issue periodically from his mouth.

When they went unanswered, he continued to travel in a generally north-easterly direction, even though it was getting progressively harder to be sure of meeting his goal! Then, just as the first doubts began to settle into his mind and he began to wonder what he would do if either his whole stratagem or his sense of direction were wrong, he heard movement ahead.

Relief turned to horror as he realised the figure making its way towards him with ferocious purpose was not an Abbas resident but, rather, another bear. And a big one too!

Quickly casting his bags aside he took his bow, cocked an arrow and aimed at the approaching creature. Realising that delay could be fatal, he fired it but, to his great disappointment realised it had missed. The bear was getting closer as he calmly cocked and fired his second arrow, this time with greater accuracy. It roared in pain but still came crashing toward him.

A third arrow also made its mark but failed to either stop or turn away the bear. Its great bulk was almost upon Aldred. He threw himself sideways in the hope that he might be able to get up and fire yet another - this time hopefully fatal - arrow, before the bear turned and attacked again.

But as he quickly got up and faced the creature he saw it, not turning, but suddenly crashing to the ground face down. Completely confused, he cautiously approached it, this time with his trusty large knife, ready to finish the bear off. Only to realise it had half a dozen arrows in its sides in addition to the ones he had hit it with.

"Well met, Aldred!" said a laughing voice, "And good shooting, even if not as effective as ours!"

Relief and comprehension poured out of Aldred as two figures stepped out of the trees some distance beyond the prostrate bear, one of whom he immediately recognised "Bharat? Is that you, Bharat? After all this time! I am so glad to see you."

"And I you, Aldred, though how you got here I cannot imagine? Thank goodness you got our attention with your whistles, though not sure using the one indicating 'Intruder' was your best choice!"

"Golly, I thought I was whistling 'Friend approaching!'" laughed Aldred, as he embraced his old friend. "But that apart, can you take me to the Abbas folk, assured I am a friend after all?"

"No problem, you intruder, you! Come this way!" and Bharat and the party led him off.

***

The journey to the new base for the renegade group did indeed take much longer than Aldred had expected, indicating that he had very clearly lost his sense of direction once within the forest. It gave him some reassurance that anyone else seeking Abbas with evil intent might get similarly lost, but in his now very weary state, he began to despair of ever arriving.

Eventually, after some hours, they started to meet more and more folk in the woods, many recognising him and waving their greeting. He was further worried, however by the lack of enthusiasm, concluding they looked almost as listless and weary as he was feeling.

When they finally entered the large clearing where the main group was gathered, he suddenly realised why. For, if the original Abbas had been a bit incomplete and rough around the edges, what met his eyes looked more like a temporary camp than a village. Tents, shacks and rudimentary shelters littered the area, with periodic campfires spotted around the place. The people looked grubby, and there was no buzz of activity, as he had expected.

Scanning around the scene before him, he spied a tired-looking Dorcas, hands on hips as she simultaneously recognised him. "Well, bless my eyes, if it isn't our spy returning! You took your time, Aldred, but well done on finding our new home."

"Home, Dorcas? It looks anything but homely to me!"

"True," she replied sadly, "but we were forced to come earlier than we had hoped. Indeed, our hope had been that we wouldn't ever need these backup lodgings but events overtook us. Those occasional sorties by Imperial Corps grew more and more frequent and, sad to say we just knew we would have to move before we were discovered."

"Well I can confirm it was a wise move, my friend. I've just left an Abbas overrun by a group of the Corps who had indeed discovered its location. They might've been a small enough group for you to have fought them off, but I'm guessing they would've been followed by larger numbers. For all the rudimentary nature of this place, it's probably a lot safer than back there. Or rather it would've been if it weren't for the news I bring you."

"I have news for you too, Aldred, but by the look on your face, yours is more urgent?"

Aldred shared his confession of finding the note with directions, but somehow losing it too. He couldn't be sure the intruders had discovered it, nor could he be certain that they could interpret either its meaning or its directions, but he was deeply worried he had given away their location and they might have to move on once again?

"Well, judging by where Bharak found you, the directions were imperfect and may well mislead them as the note misled you, old friend. I think we have some time. I also think the people are in no fit state to travel, not to mention that we have nowhere obvious or prepared to move to! My instinct is to preserve our energies for now, and defend our space if they come."

"Well, you're the leader, Dorcas, and as always I respect your judgement. I'm worried, but you know your situation and your folk better than I."

"Good. So we've got time for my news. I have someone for you to meet."

"That'd be lovely, though I would be most grateful to see Mahanda and Sharla first - assuming they are still amongst you?"

"Oh, don't worry," she laughed, "not only are they still here, but they are with the person I want to take you to. Come on, they're over here, deeper into our settlement."

They walked over, while Dorcas briefed Bharak and the others to prepare the lookouts to be especially on their guards in case of further, less welcome intruders. As they walked, Aldred realised his first impressions about the roughness of the settlement had been generally correct but he could see that it was taking shape, and the resilience of the Abbas folk was still evident. He could also see how widespread the developing village was; not surprising really as it had to accommodate the same number of folk as their former habitation. In the middle was a large circular area, cleared of trees and sporting a rather impressive rectangular wooden building. Clearly a Meeting House had been built, and in all probability in advance of their translocation there.

Not far from this was another, smaller building that Aldred guessed was probably where the sick were cared for. His worrying began anew as he was guided towards it and began to fear the worst for those he loved. But a quick look at Dorcas' grinning face quickly reassured him that his fears were misplaced.

Word of their approach had apparently reached the Sick House as, a hundred strides before they reached it, the door was suddenly thrown open and a figure rushed out, followed shyly, by a younger person. As soon as he recognised her, Aldred too began to run and, as they met, he swept Mahanda up in his arms. To whoops of delight from all within sight, he held her, kissed and hugged her tightly.

"Well, you took your time, husband!" she said, laughingly through her tears as she hugged and kissed him back.

"I was delayed a bit," he replied a little sheepishly, "I encountered a bit of bother and ..."

"I know. I heard!" she smiled and kissed him again.

"But how could you hear? I mean ...?" he started to reply, but she interrupted him. "You'll see. You'll see," she said mysteriously. "But first you need to be reunited with Sharla."

Looking up, Aldred then recognised the younger person with his wife, but who stood hesitantly by the door. "By golly, Sharla, you have grown!" he exclaimed.

"Well it has been nearly three years, Aldred!" scolded Mahanda. "I did, I think, already say it's been a while! You didn't expect your daughter to stay the same for such a long time, did you?" She laughed again.

He laughed in response and said, "What, even if you've stayed as young and beautiful as ever in the interim?"

"Hello, father!" said the teenager. But she stayed standing awkwardly there until Aldred swept her into his arms too, saying, "Oh, Sharla it has been too, too long. I am so glad to see you, and so very pleased you're ok. I feel like I left behind a wee girl and find I'm returning to a young woman! Oh ...!" and he was lost for words.

"Sorry to interrupt this touching reunion, but I think your wife and daughter have someone else for you to meet," said Dorcas, leading the threesome, arms linked together as if nothing could ever separate them again, inside the Sick House.

It was virtually empty apart from a few cots, on one of which was sitting someone Aldred had also not seen for quite some time. He stopped still in absolute shock and relief, eventually bellowing one single word. One single name: "Luke?"

Then, quieter but just as shocked, "How the heck? How did you find your way here? I thought ... I thought you were maybe done for, though I knew you'd not been killed in the spider run ... and I hoped ... I hoped that ... but..." and again his incoherent words ran into silence.

With a broad smile the lad on the cot with his leg in wooden splints simply replied, "Well, it's a bit of a long story, to be honest. You see …"

Once more Dorcas interrupted. "Can I suggest that poor Aldred has a chance to get his breath back first, not to mention a meal? He looks a shadow of his former self and, poor though our accommodation here in Forest Abbas is, there is food and we folk don't want him to feel we've lost our sense of hospitality!

"Come on, Aldred, let Mahanda take you over to her home and give you an opportunity to wash, change and join us for supper and story-telling. Luke is strong enough to walk across to the Meeting House these days, and we can eat and share."

"Well I have to admit that a wash wouldn't go amiss, Dorcas. I mean I think I probably, um …"

"Stink is the word, beloved," said a laughing Mahanda. "Come on, there's a brilliant washing place by a large stream near my … our … home. And while you're there, I can get you some more clothes. You can tell I had faith you'd return, as I hung onto them!"

20 STORIES AND REUNIONS

An hour or so later, Aldred was led on to the Meeting House where he was able to enjoy the best meal he had eaten in probably a year: freshwater fish, vegetables and some more wonderful, freshly-baked bread.

"How do you get flour here?" he enquired and was told that there was a certain amount of trading with village settlements some days beyond the forest edge, though they were treated with a degree of suspicion. However, under the guise of itinerant trappers from Ruark, Abbas folk were able to exchange mountain and forest produce with food from the villages. It seemed a bit of a risk to their security, but when he bit into the bread, Aldred couldn't help but feel it was worth it!

As they ate, they shared their stories since last they had separated on that fateful day when dusk and spiders had threatened. Aldred realised as Dorcas started that it wasn't just bread he had been missing, but the wonderful story-telling of the Abbas folk. They would never let an opportunity for a lengthy saga pass or replace it with a short synopsis, so he had to settle down for the whole tale before finally hearing how Luke had been rescued!

"Some months before we left Abbas, one of our residents - the blacksmith Brusca - accused a younger man of abusing his daughter. Naturally we believed him, as the girl supported his claims so we exiled him, warning him that if he ever returned his life would be forfeit.

"Then, during the transfer of the community to this location, one of our groups was attacked by a group of large wild cats."

"Luke and I were also attacked by such a group," interrupted Aldred.

"Yes, we suspect it was probably part of the same pride." said Dorcas. "Our folk drove them off but, in the process Brusca was sorely injured, and died soon afterwards. Which left us without a blacksmith, but released the young lady, Portha by name, from the influence of her father. While she was being comforted over his loss, she admitted that a great injustice had been meted out to the young man who had been accused and exiled.

"She shocked the woman supporting her with the news that it had in fact been her own father who had beaten her because he didn't approve of her choice of partner. Brusca had then made up the rape allegations to cover his own behaviour and to get rid of Callan. News was brought to me, and even in the midst of the chaos of settling in Forest Abbas, I dispatched a group of young men to seek poor Callan, right the wrong that had been meted out to him and see whether he could be restored to the community?"

Aldred was beginning to become frustrated by the convoluted and lengthy tale which seemed to have absolutely no connection with Luke's rescue. He knew better though, than to interrupt, musing to himself how different such a community that loved story-telling was from one with Forgetter roots, which saw tales and the past as a threat.

"Sadly," Dorcas continued, "we never found Callan and the injustice meted out to him remains as a stain on our community. However, the group searching for him heard cries for help from another young man, injured and trapped down in a giant spider run!"

"Aha!" exclaimed Aldred, "so that's how you got out!"

"Absolutely!" piped up Luke. "And boy was it awful getting out with my twisted leg and …"

Dorcas silenced him with a look, and then castigated him for telling the story out of sequence. She did, though, allow him to track back a touch in time to tell how he had battled single-handedly with the spider. Clearly this was a tale that the Abbas folk loved to hear and which had already become a community favourite, as Luke told it with embellishments evidencing a much-told story! Again Aldred thought to himself: how far the young man had come since his roots in Coldharbour!

Luke continued, describing how he lay in the dark without his spear, then forced himself to his feet, prepared to fight the creature bare-handed (clearly an addition to the story that Luke had found made a good climax, Aldred guessed, though he was far too kind to say so!)

"Come on then, beastie," Luke said, "Come and get me!"

"But instead of a second giant spider belting along the run," Dorcas reported, "suddenly there were two faces peering over the edge from above, enquiring how he'd known they were there to come and get him?"

And the whole audience, including Luke and Aldred rolled around with laughter, at the humorous and frankly miraculous conclusion to the tale!

All were delighted to hear Aldred's addition to the story, as he told of his return to the run after finding Abbas abandoned, and how he had found the body of the spider the following day. Nobody had ever heard of anybody killing one of the ferocious creatures before; Luke was quite pleased that there was confirmation that he had indeed achieved this and it wasn't just a tale. However, the suggestion that his new name might be

'Spider-slayer' did not excite Luke quite as much as it might have done!

The story continued: how they had managed to bandage up his leg, which fortunately wasn't broken though he had been unable to stand on it. With the rescuers' assistance and a makeshift pair of crutches Luke had been able to travel to the Abbas folks' new base. It had been a long and difficult journey, and during it he had also become increasingly unwell. The scratches from the battle with the cats had become infected. By the time they had reached the forest settlement, he had become feverish and had eventually collapsed into unconsciousness. Long treatment and the best of their rudimentary medical care had been needed to nurse him back to health. As Aldred had arrived, Luke was at long last back to nearly full strength and mobilising well.

Luke chided Aldred for not having ever said that he was married or that the young girl he claimed to have 'discovered' to have Mage gifts was in fact his own daughter.

Aldred replied, "Ah well, I didn't want to put her and my wife in danger by sharing the whole tale."

"And you lectured me on trust and faith!" replied Luke, and they both chuckled.

In that shared laughter, Aldred realised that he was, it seemed, forgiven for not returning to rescue his charge. Their mutual bond was tightened further in that moment. He also felt that perhaps the experience had matured Luke somewhat. He seemed less reactionary and more thoughtful. Funny how experiences of suffering and survival sometimes make one stronger, he thought.

It was now Aldred's turn to share his own adventures: how he had reached Abbas, only to find it abandoned and thus unable to get anyone to help him, his period of recuperation, and the discovery of Mahanda's coded note. In true Abbas style, he embellished the story of being disturbed by the scouting group of Imperial Corps, evading them by the skin of his teeth and eventually escaping. By prior agreement with Dorcas, he did not share that he had lost the note, reasoning this detail would only add unnecessary worry at this time to a community already under pressure.

He told of his period at Offwell and how eventually, after the hospitality, care and attention of Ellen and her husband, he had eventually received the second part of Mahanda's message, with directions to Forest Abbas.

By the end of the evening, with all events caught up, both Aldred and Dorcas looked across the gathered community, complete (apart from the scouts and lookouts necessary to keep the place safe) and expressed belief that their reunion had been a morale booster. It reminded them all that though they were a group of people from very different backgrounds, whose only uniting factor was a conflict or disagreement with the ways of the Empire, they had somehow melded together into a group with a common cause. Their flight from Abbas had taken a huge toll, but this evening of story-telling and sharing had emboldened them, reminding them that they also had a purpose and could believe in their future together.

Luke, coming from a Forgetter background, where history and story were frowned upon, and even hints of magery despised, added how much he had treasured the story-telling and the company of folks tolerant of people with strange gifts. He promised that if his own were of any use to them, he would be at their disposal, assuming they could work out how.

It was agreed that there would be a community meeting the following evening to discuss the future. In the meantime Aldred was sent home with his family. Though Luke was invited to join them, he returned to his cot in the Sick House. "For now, it's where I'm comfortable. And I don't want to interrupt your family reunion," he joked.

Shortly after he'd arrived in the Sick House, Sharla knocked and came in. "It's ok, Sharla, I don't need any care tonight. I just need sleep."

"Fine, I need sleep, too. I'm going into one of the other cots at the far end if that's ok with you? I decided, like you, I'd best not interrupt the my parents' reunion, either!"

Within minutes they were both sleeping soundly.

***

In the morning, refreshed and re-energised, Aldred met with Dorcas and several of the Elders, some of whom drifted in and out as they took off for periods of lookout duty. Aldred was able to share some of his observations of activity in the Empire during his scouting exercises prior to his flight to Coldharbour, plus what he had learnt while in Offwell. Clearly, some of these were by now a year or so out of date, but he reasoned that the pattern had been developing for some time and this was confirmed by what he had learnt from Ellen about the way things had been developing across the Empire.

Central control had been increasing as the levels of wealth in the capital had risen, resulting in increasing demands on the provinces, and in turn upon the more distant settlements, to offer more and more in terms of food and supplies. The need to overcome the villagers' understandable reluctance and sometimes inability to contribute more had resulted in recruitment of more members of the Corps. This in turn had meant firstly greater demands with more military mouths to feed, and secondly a more heavy-handed approach to the collections of supplies.

"In essence the whole system is developing into an increasingly oppressive dictatorship," Aldred explained, "with villages near the capital reduced to near starvation and groups of Corps travelling farther and farther in search of new sources of food. I don't think they were specifically seeking us as as they reached Abbas, just reaching further from the centre when they stumbled upon us? My fear is that if they did find us, not only would they demand unreasonable amounts from our already meagre supplies, but if they had a Seeker amongst them, they would sense those with magery and take them too.

"I think you have been wise to have decamped here in the face of those threats, though I can see that the outlook is not good. You were barely subsisting in Abbas. I fear you will struggle even more here in the forest encampment, not least because you have been forced to move earlier than expected. Your shelters are even poorer here than there, and food supplies are even more limited. At least we had cottage gardens there, with fruit and vegetables growing. Here, it'll take months to produce anything - and we're entering the worst winter months!"

"So what do you suggest?" one of the Elders asked.

"My instincts, as you know, are generally peaceful," replied Aldred, thoughtfully, "but I am beginning to wonder: do we somehow need to lead some element of resistance?"

"Seriously?" responded Dorcas. "We're a settlement of only fifty or so adults. We couldn't take on even a single group of armed, trained soldiers, leave alone the combined might of the whole Corps!"

"Oh I wasn't suggesting we go it alone. Maybe we could foment resistance among other groups and villages ..."

"Well, that didn't go too well in the past for the northern folk in Ruark, or for the Islanders, did it? And there were many more of them than us!"

"True - but perhaps their motivation wasn't as strong as ours will be in the current situation?" suggested Aldred.

Dorcas was dismissive. "Their independence was fierce and strongly defended, yet they were defeated by the magery of the Empire!"

"But that was when the Empire was being founded by Mages working together with unity of gifts and purpose. Camrin and Magrat have removed all Mages who could threaten them, but in the process, they have have also disposed of any serious magery-support that they might have garnered. They depend on their personal magery at home, and on brute force elsewhere. Perhaps that is a weakness we can exploit? I mean, can we seriously seek to survive simply by hiding all the time?"

"Hiding has worked so far," suggested another of the Elders, "and I for one don't have much of an appetite for battle! Also, those with magery gifts amongst us are all pretty weak, and hardly likely to threaten the power of the Emperor?"

With the subject of hiding having arisen, Aldred enquired if Luke had shared his experience of unusual magery gifts with the community? It transpired that he had remained true to his Forgetter roots and never even mentioned them - no surprise there. His mention of gifts the previous night had been the first hint.

This in turn led to a discussion about how Luke's gifts might in any way be helpful. They had established that he might make a small number of people Unseen amazingly effectively, but it seemed doubtful that he could make a whole community, plus their settlement, invisible! It appeared once again a minor benefit, but hardly a game-changer?

At this point in the debate, they were interrupted by news from lookouts. Two people had been spotted approaching the forest edge who appeared to be approaching Forest Abbas. They were apparently being careful to proceed as furtively as possible, but their direction of travel was purposeful, almost as if they knew exactly where they were heading.

Dorcas suspended the meeting as she took several of the Elders and a few other villagers to investigate the situation, so Aldred went to spend some time catching up with Luke, who was gingerly trying to walk with crutches and without his splints. They walked and talked and shared their hopes and fears, as old friends and comrades sometimes do.

At one point, Luke said, "Aldred, have you ever heard of 'books'?"

"Oh yes, they're a sort of recording of the words of the ancients from the Great Age, I believe. A way of sharing their wisdom, I understand, though we have struggled to decipher them."

"Did you know they had some here, perhaps sixty or so, and that some of the folk have been working on translating them?"

"Well, yes, but I don't think they have got very far with that, have they?"

"Amazingly, since you've been away, they think they have made a breakthrough. Apparently one of the collection they had dismissed as a childish picture book had symbols and images that gave clues for how those symbols of writing sound. There are 26 of these symbols, starting with A with a picture of an apple. They guessed this meant the symbol had an 'A' sound, and moved on from there.

"Many of the images were of things that nobody could recognise - the 'E' sound apparently begins a word for a strange creature called an 'elephant,' which looks as scary as those giant spiders! But there were enough recognisable images with sufficient symbols to start compiling an initial list of sounds. Then, when they looked in other books, they found short words that made sense with the symbols they had got, and if they then went to bigger words that meant something to us, they could work out other sounds.

"It turned out to be more complicated than that - some symbols seem to have no sound sometimes - some had slightly different sounds in different words. But after a while they found they could read quite a lot of the books."

"That's amazing, Luke! I think the Abbas folk had always believed books were important and could be useful. It's a shame that during the Forgetter ages people felt they were all tainted by the past atrocities of the Great Age, and had to be destroyed! Have they learnt anything helpful to us, do you know?"

"I'm afraid it's very early days. I'm too new to the community to have important stuff shared with me, and remember I have been pretty poorly for most of my time here. It's just that Rose, one of the older women caring for me, was one of the group who had been working on the books, and she told me about it as I got better, as part of letting me know how Abbas works."

"So what is in these books, then?"

"Well, they seem to be different types: some useful, others less so. Some are factual - one showed all about people's bodies - anatomy apparently is the word - with pictures and descriptions of how we are put together. The healers were really interested in what they could learn from those. Others seem to be, well stories I suppose. Some are really complex and very, very confusing, since they are telling tales of a period that is beyond our comprehension. Many of the words can be read but mean absolutely nothing to us, so it is really difficult to understand the whole story."

"So no real use to us?"

"Maybe not, but they do give a picture of life as it was in the past. And you did say that we can learn a lot from history, so maybe with time we can learn more that could be useful."

"Conceivably, though we'll have to deal with our present problems first, I suspect!"

"Oh yes, there is loads of work to do, and I get the impression it's not considered a priority! Mind you, there is one book that is really fun - a story of magery and battles between Mages - though not like ours. They seem to need to wave wooden sticks and say special words and the book tells of a great battle of good versus evil and great and good Mages called Harry and Hermin. It seems to be a series and nearly the whole story has been kept!"

"Sounds interesting but to be honest, useless to me? I am disappointed - I had hoped there could be more to learn from books."

"Well maybe, Aldred but, as you say, if we can get past our current challenges, they may yet prove useful"

They walked (and limped) on a while in silence, then Luke said, "Oh, another thing there was one book actually two copies with slightly different words but clearly telling the same story, a set of stories, from a period long before the Great Age. Many are really mysterious and a lot of it makes no sense at all. It's almost like they are fantasy stories but also have moral lessons to teach. Rose says they think they might be somehow to do with religious beliefs, as a lot of the stories connect with a being they call God or 'The Lord'."

"I thought you Forgetters were as passionately against religions as you are against magery?" laughed Aldred.

"Oh yes, my instincts are that it's all stuff and nonsense! Though, strangely, Rose said it's her favourite of all the books. She says it's got loads of really interesting and perplexing stories, with exciting adventures and great heroes. Terrible people too, like a King who was so threatened by the birth of a baby he'd heard was born in a certain village, that he sent his soldiers there to murder all the children under two!"

"Sounds a little like sending Seekers to betray Mages to the Emperor?" said Aldred, sadly. "Some things never seem to change!"

"I had the same thought," replied Luke. "But some of the stories were really inspiring, and in the evenings, when she was taking a turn looking after me when I was poorly, she read me bits and I really enjoyed them. After community meals together, sometimes she tells them too. Says she's convinced we could learn a lot from this particular book, given time, without having to buy into the 'is there a God or not' angle."

"Well, maybe, Luke. But as I say, I think we have more important things to consider, and I'm not sure that books or Gods will be much help at the moment!"

"As so often, Aldred, you may well be right, though some of the lessons taught might prove useful and I intend to spend some time with Rose learning more, when I can? Anyway, we shall see!"

They walked on, enjoying the opportunity to catch up and avoiding the one subject that bothered them most, about Marsha and what had happened to her. Eventually, they circled back at the Meeting House and sought something to eat.

But, not long afterwards, a grinning Dorcas arrived, announcing, "Well, well, Aldred, this seems to be a week for reunions!"

Aldred and Luke stood up but, as they saw who accompanied Dorcas, both nearly fell over again. To their joint incredible delight, there stood a shy-looking young man and, glory of glory, Marsha!

After rubbing his eyes in amazement, Luke hobbled and hopped across to her and, almost hyperventilating, threw his arms around her. "I thought … I feared I'd never see you again! You … oh Marsha .. I thought I'd lost you forever and I …" and then he just hugged her and wept.

Aldred joined in the hugs and they danced up and down making joyful whooping noises for words were impossible to express their feelings.

Eventually they settled down and Marsha was able to introduce the slightly sheepish-looking Callan who was even more embarrassed when Marsha praised him publicly for saving her life, keeping her clothed and fed and being an all round saviour. She had agreed this stratagem in advance with him to reinforce the fact that she had been quite safe him, but her excessive praise was way more than he had expected.

Dorcas, practical as ever, suggested lunch be brought. There would be an opportunity to catch up before the community meeting due after lunch.

What a joyful meal it was as they each told their tales breathlessly, with eyes open and mouths wide in wonder! Many of the stories shared the previous evening were repeated, this time with the addition of Marsha and Callan's adventures. She shared her theory that somehow her magery was to augment, focus and strengthen not just Luke's ability to be Unseen, but also the gifts of others. Thus together she and Callan had travelled in the general direction of Forest Abbas. Then, as they got closer, they had focussed their minds in conjunction, enhancing Callan's ability to heard peoples' thoughts, until they were able to sense exactly where the community was.

The original plan had been that Marsha would approach alone and negotiate a safe return for Callan. They reached a point where it was too close for him to travel with her safely any more and agreed this would be their rendezvous spot. Then that night, before settling down for sleep, Callan had suggested they might work magery together one more time to check if Portha was still in the community. He reasoned that if she were, she might be able to speak in his defence and if not, then, frankly he had no wish to rejoin the settlement. In that case, he would set out to find a village where he could settle and support himself as a tanner. Though he no longer wished to live alone, he felt he couldn't go back to a community where pain was such a part of his unhealed memories.

As they sat and focused together, Callan sent out his mind-scan, now far better developed during their travels together, until he found he could settle it on Portha's mind. He wasn't too good, he admitted, in reading minds, but he could pick up general thoughts, he supposed, plus vague feelings. When he found her, it transpired that Portha's mind was just a jumble of hopeful emotions and, amazingly, images of him, Callan! It was incomprehensible but that had been enough to convince him and Marsha that it was safe for them to return together.

The last few days of journeying, took them straight to where they now knew the settlement to be and, once they reached the cover of the trees, they had openly hailed the lookouts they knew would be hiding there. To their great relief, they had been greeted as friends and, with Callan reassured that he was no longer an exile, Dorcas had accompanied them to the camp.

With all the stories to share, it was a miracle that anyone ate anything! But somehow, by the time they had all caught up, the food that had arrived on the table had all disappeared, ready for the community meeting to follow.

21 PLANS

Marsha and Luke were amazed to be able to attend the community meeting, as in Coldharbour, the Elders met separately and later informed the people of their decisions. In Abbas it was much more inclusive, although it was noticeable that giving everyone a voice meant the debate did meander around rather a lot. There were many words, a lot of grumbling and, frankly, very little by way of decisions. Though all agreed that the situation since the newcomers had arrived had added options to their armoury, there was scepticism about Aldred's idea of fomenting rebellion across the Empire. Many felt that it would make Abbas more of a target to be tracked down and destroyed. Bharat suggested that they might move again - this time northwards to the mountainous areas of Ruark. However, many who had either visited there before or traded with the northern folk suggested it would be even harder to survive there than in the woods of northern Southfleet - and that was paving hard enough!

Overall the majority remained in the 'hide and survive' camp, especially as they now had the option of Luke and Marsha making the Mages Unseen.

Dorcas judged that this was the right time to reveal that Aldred had mislaid the message from Mahanda which potentially could have given their locality away, but again the consensus was that it had been coded in such a way that only her husband could have understood. As it had transpired, even he had taken weeks to understand it! Dorcas was confident that, even if it had been discovered, at best it would only give a general hint of visiting Offwell, and she trusted Ellen not to pass on the additional directions. Additionally, as they got deeper into winter, wasn't it an unlikely time for the Imperial forces to be travelling around much, especially in these northern areas?

Dorcas and the meeting felt reassured that they had time to prepare (although it was not quite clear what they would be preparing for!) and the gathering gradually lost momentum and urgency. It was agreed, though that they would continue to make the settlement more fit for purpose as a place to settle in for the medium term, or at least for the winter. Rotas were to be worked out for hunting, construction and lookout duties - and Aldred was charged with assessing and training those with magery gifts, to see what those within the community could now offer, augmented as they would be by Luke, Marsha and Callan and their insights.

As he looked around the hall, Luke couldn't help but feel a little jealous how Callan was sitting comfortably and affectionally next to Portha. He wondered if he would ever do that with Marsha, or whether her role and seriousness would once again dominate her approach to life, as in their earlier period together with Aldred.

He realised that he had never developed any techniques for talking with members of the opposite sex; his focus in Coldharbour had been on fishing and Feeling (not to mention dung-collecting!) and since they had left, mostly on survival. He also realised that his self-obsession had not exactly enamoured him to Marsha and he resolved that his sulking needed to stop. As he thought that, he realised that having a purpose over the last few weeks, even in the face of significant challenges, had lightened his mood and generally overcome this tendency all by itself.

He then wondered if he might seek to develop the skills of courtship, as well as of magery while they spent future sessions with Aldred. After all if he had learnt one thing in the past few months, it was patience - something he reassured himself could prove useful!

He had little time to wonder further as he was shepherded out of the Meeting House by Aldred with Marsha, Callan, Sharla and three other folk he hadn't met yet. As they walked some distance to find a suitable place to work in, two men in their twenties introduced themselves as Arkan and Tam, and a proud-looking older woman, as Iffley.

They each shared what magery gifts they had, beginning with Iffley. Apparently she was a moderately powerful Porter, who had once held a senior role in the palace until Magrat suffered a fit of paranoia and started to suspect she was plotting against her. Iffley had shared her concerns with Aldred, and had been with him, Mahanda and Sharla when they had decided to escape from the capital, eventually settling with them among the folk of Abbas. During Aldred's absence, Iffley had schooled Sharla's gifts since she, too, was a Porter and the two women had developed an impressive level of combined magery.

Arkan and Tam originally hailed from a Forgetter village near the wastelands, where big, ancient cities had once been. They had grown up as neighbours together and formed a mental Pather bond from childhood. They had managed to keep their link secret until a Seeker had found them out, but deemed them too low-level to be a threat to the Empire. However, once their gifts had been discovered, they were treated with deep and threatening suspicion by their fellow villagers. Eventually they had decided to leave and seek a life together, away from their home. Over time and after much travelling, they had encountered a group of dissatisfied renegades who accepted them into their party, eventually ending up among the Abbas community. Individually they had weak Pathic abilities but had found that if they worked together, they were much more effective and they could not only read minds but could also block others from reading theirs.

Marsha explained that her gifts seemed to be as an augmenter of others' magery. She wondered if she might be able to work with this pair, plus with Callan, who was clearly a Pather too. Perhaps, together, they could develop into an even more powerful team?

"Hold on there!" said Aldred, "Perhaps we're getting ahead of ourselves? Let's start with what we can do alone initially, and hone our skills?" And it was agreed this would be a good way forward.

***

The next weeks were interesting, even enjoyable, as the group worked together, shared together and learnt to work as a team. As members of the community, they also had to contribute to village life. Callan rejoined his father in working shifts tanning hides and they recruited Luke, officially as the tanners' assistant, though almost all of his role was to collect a vital ingredient in their work: villagers' urine, necessary for the tanning process. Luke joked that it was perhaps one step up from being a Dung Man! But frankly it was a much more pleasant job than that and, if he was honest, rather easier work than the other roles on offer. He could also occasionally join the hunting and fishing patrols which were a helpful diversion from other duties.

Marsha joined the foraging parties and, together with Callan, worked some shifts on lookout duties, honing their skills in Far-Seeing together beyond the limits of their eyesight, so killing two birds with the same stone. Arkan, Tam, Sharla and Iffley, meanwhile, carried on with their normal tasks and duties in between sessions with Aldred.

Under Aldred's tutelage they each found ways of maximising their magery skills individually, developing confidence and consistency. The later stage was even more useful as they joined for sessions of training and exploration of their gifts together, experimenting with different combinations of augmentation and collaboration. Aldred was particularly impressed how their originality revealed new and exciting aspects that he had not encountered before. Callan, for instance questioned why he couldn't Path Marsha's mind and, after some investigation, Aldred identified that she appeared to have an unconscious blocking ability. With practice she could do it intentionally - and Sharla, who it also transpired had some previously undiscovered augmenting ability, could enhance this further, giving the team another useful defensive skill.

The delights and surprises of this period together were many, binding them together into a powerful magery team. Not only did they learn to work together, they also bonded as a group of friends, despite their different backgrounds and ages, and began to socialise together in their spare time. Callan produced some wonderful new leather clothes for Luke, which were much more comfortable than other people's cast-offs. They also matched those worn by Callan and Marsha, exhibiting not only his phenomenal leather-working skills, but also his remarkable eye for design. The rest of the magery team were so complimentary that over time he produced matching outfits for them too, prompting admiring, not to mention jealous glances from the other Abbas folk.

Luke and Marsha loved spending evenings hearing stories - particularly when the old lady Rose came and joined them to share tales from her favourite book. Often the stories would lead to stimulating discussions about how the God they referred to seemed to relate to the characters in the tales. The group generally agreed that the existence of some guiding deity was ludicrous However, some found many aspects of the God in question were strangely attractive.

Sharla expressed huge scepticism about some of the godly interventions reported, particularly in the early stories. "I mean," she said, "that story of the great flood is ridiculous. How could humanity be all wiped out in one fell sweep and then repopulate the world with such a small group of people? They'd have the same in-breeding problems of Luke and Marsha's community, wouldn't they?"

"I suppose so." replied Callan. "Though maybe it, and many of the other stories are a sort of community myth? Possibly they understood the flood as a judgement, just as I reckon people could say the great floods and wars that ended the Great Age were actions of this God. I mean, obviously it was people who set off those wars and the ensuing carnage but you could argue that God was fed up with humanity's behaviour and let them destroy themselves!"

Iffley laughed and said, "Then he's a pretty incompetent God, in my opinion, if he is a destructive sort! After all, we and thousands of others are still here. Not only that, the Emperors are still doing some pretty foul things. So the situation has hardly improved!"

"I think you've got a point there, Iffley." replied Sharla. "Which is, I suppose, what I was trying to explore. I just wonder if the people who believed in this God had a relationship that was, I don't know, distant and uncertain? So that they saw godly action in some things that were sometimes nothing to do with God at all? I mean, humans are a pretty stubborn lot and are easily led off the track?"

"A bit like sheep?" piped in Marsha.

"How so?" asked Callan.

"Well, one of the images that Rose has mentioned several times is of the people as sheep and this God as a shepherd. The teacher in the later bits that Luke likes so much even refers to himself as a good shepherd. One of my jobs in Coldharbour was to take a turn looking after the sheep. You can lead them, guide them, encourage them but, believe me, sometimes they simply will not do what you want them to do. You do the best you can and hope that's enough, leaving them sometimes to make their own mistakes. I wonder if that is the way the writer is trying to portray the relationship between this deity and the people?"

Tam was very dismissive of the stories, which he felt were too fantastical on the one hand and, frankly included many characters who were, not to put to fine a point on it, hardly admirable heroes!

Arkan, as usual, agreed, but Sharla suggested that, surprisingly she felt she learnt as much from their mistakes as from the actions they might have or should have taken?

"I mean, take those Samson stories? He could have done so much better with the abilities he had, but messed up pretty much completely. I wonder if it might encourage us, as people with gifts to use them effectively?"

"Perhaps we could tell that to Camrin?" joked Luke, and they all laughed uproariously.

When they had settled down a bit, Callan said, "Going back to that relationship idea, I do find the understanding of a God with a loving and supportive commitment to the people quite attractive. Inspiring even. It seems to me that communication with Gods, if they do exist, is not easy and yeah, a bit like humans and sheep! So I just don't think those ancient storytellers could completely work out what was going on."

Sharla nodded. "Perhaps that's why they wrote all the stories down? Hoping that one day they might work out the whole story." she suggested.

"Well that's going well, after all this time!" said Iffley, causing much laughter again.

For Luke and Marsha, though, it was the teaching and stories in the latter sections of the book that most intrigued and excited them. They would spend long hours of their leisure time talking about them, exploring their opaque and yet encouraging meanings. Luke particularly enjoyed finding himself in such stimulating conversations with Marsha as an equal, though he sometimes lay in bed wondering how he might some day turn their conversations away from past teachings, towards a more personal relationship ...

Aldred was pleased that his two companions, who had always previously seemed rather at loggerheads with each other, were now getting along so well. He was even more surprised how the pair, despite their Forgetter heritage, seemed to be loving these old stories and engaging so well with the discussions of history.

Overall it was a thoroughly stimulating and enjoyable period which took them happily through the winter months. For Aldred, Marsha, Callan and Luke it was the longest period of peace and security that they had experienced for quite some time.

Sadly, it wasn't to last.

22 UNDER ATTACK

Spring arrived, gradually breaking through the frosty endgame of a cold and challenging winter. Food had been hard to come by, but the community had worked hard to gather what could be foraged. Overall, even though most had lost some weight, the folk had been fed just about enough, and there was a growing sense of optimism. Several times wild animals had arrived in the vicinity, and on all occasions had been effectively driven off by magery without force of arms. The first attack, a pair of bears, was warded off by Arkan and Tam, reinforced by Marsha; they had simply driven them off by sending negative warning thoughts at the beasts.

The second incursion was not so straightforward, but a combination of the threesome had caused another large group of hungry, hunting cats to hesitate, though they hadn't moved away. Then Iffley had thrown some Porter force at them. The leading cat was briefly repelled before Marsha then spontaneously added her augmenting powers to Iffley, and the results were surprisingly powerful: the two leading lionesses were literally lifted off their feet and thrown backwards, colliding with those behind them. Fear and confusion overtook the creatures and they ran off, deciding presumably to hunt somewhere safer!

The hunters held in reserve behind the magery team cheered and lowered their bows in relief and surprise at how effectively the animals had been driven off. But it was Aldred who was most impressed by the almost accidental discovery that Marsha could augment two gifts simultaneously - even more so when he realised that she had been communicating with Callan mentally at the same time.

Sharla had not been present, so Aldred implemented some more training sessions with the group soon afterwards to explore how she and Marsha might jointly augment several magery styles at the same time, whilst remaining in communication telepathically. The results were very impressive: not only was everything magnified almost exponentially, but Marsha was able to share Callan's gifts amongst the whole team throughout the exercises. They were all able to communicate with each other as they worked together, making their magery much more coordinated.

Over time, Aldred was able to finally ascertain Luke's 'hidden' gift, which he'd not been able to work out before: an ability to resist magery gifts thrown at him. If Iffley threw a Porting force at him that would normally knock him over, he could easily absorb the blow. If Marsha augmented the force but Sharla augmented Luke, the effect was the same. It worked just as well with Pathic attacks, and it was hoped, would do likewise against Melding. Aldred was also rather pleased to find that if the Mages were all being made Unseen, he not only couldn't see or smell them, he couldn't sense their presence with his Seeker gifts. They were truly hidden!

Luke, though, was finding these discoveries somewhat underwhelming; he had secretly hoped his hidden ability might be a little more glamorous and impressive. Being able to hide had seemed rather boring in the first place and the discovery that he could also fend off attacks wasn't the most thrilling of his life - he had rather dreamt of being able to contribute rather more.

Sensing Luke's frustration, Aldred instituted a series of exercises with both Marsha and Sharla enhancing his gift. Together they could successfully make the whole community Unseen and on one occasion a hunting party arrived back to find the place apparently completely deserted of people. Their faces were a picture when, miraculously, they all reappeared at once!

Nevertheless, poor Luke couldn't overcome his instinctive feeling that this pretty passive gift boiled down still to simply hiding. Very clever and effective hiding, but it felt a rather unimpressive ability.

One evening, he expressed this to Marsha a little grumpily. She initially responded that it could still prove terribly useful - and what was important surely, was that, as a team they each contributed something useful? "Not to mention that your absorbing gift can protect us all! A soldier needs a shield as well as a sword after all!"

While this didn't exactly reassure Luke, it prompted her to ask Aldred to see if she and Sharla could jointly enhance Luke's and Callan's far-seeing ability, which they had almost forgotten about in their exercises.

The timing could not have been more perfect; the next day Aldred gathered the four of them during a break between their duties, for as they sent their thoughts out widely together, they identified a large band of thirty or so humans marching together in the direction of Forest Abbas. Using Luke's image of the group, they were able to work out that they were a group of Imperial Corps. When Callan scanned the leader's mind for intentions, it became clear how good Aldred's tutelage was - he could ascertain that the scouts had visited one of the villages the Abbas folk traded with and were aware that there was a community living north of them within the forest.

Being a part of the teamwork that was able to give the community such information and warning, well in advance of anything the lookouts would have been able to offer, reassured Luke that his gifts weren't simply passive, after all.

Dorcas was summoned and the villagers were able to prepare for the Corps' arrival. Older folk and children were escorted further into the forest to a place of relative safety, and the remaining folk gathered in the settlement, in line with their agreed defence plans.

Lookouts reported over the next couple of days on the progress of the party of soldiers as they came closer and closer to the settlement. It had been hoped that they might be too hard to discover by random searching but, too late, they realised that there was a Seeker among the group who was clearly far-sensing the Mages amongst the Abbas folk and leading the Corps straight to the village.

The magery team went into action to implement the first part of the plan: to hide all occupants of Abbas, using Luke's augmented gifts. When the soldiers arrived, they looked around, somewhat perplexed, at an apparently occupied village with no people evident. The Seeker amongst them consulted with the leader, telling him that until a short time ago there had been considerable numbers right here, including Mages, but that, suddenly, there was nobody there.

The strange thing for the Abbas folk was that they remained visible to each other, and could easily step aside when the solders passed where they had been standing.

Marsha and the Pathers together tried to instil the idea of leaving but it had no effect on the soldiers, even when Sharla sought to enhance the message. The Abbas folk realised they had not completely thought through their plan. Disappointment turned into distress when the captain decided to order his men to start destroying the settlement, beginning with the Meeting House.

As one soldier approached it with a torch lit from one of the village fires, one of the Abbas villagers stopped him in his tracks by stabbing him with a spear. To the members of the Corps he simply appeared to clutch his abdomen and drop dead; though it must have been terrifying to watch, they were soldiers, trained for combat and immediately drew their weapons.

Trained or not, though, they had no defence against invisible foes and, one by one, they were cut down in minutes flat. When Luke relaxed his Unseen magery, they were all, though, horrified by the scene of carnage before them.

Nobody spoke for a while as they considered the enormity of what they had just done. In many ways it felt like an enormous achievement: to have taken a first step against an Empire which each, in their own ways, had reasons to oppose.

Nevertheless, what they had done simply appalled them. They were not soldiers; neither were they rebels, as had become evident when Aldred had suggested counter-insurgency as a tactic.

They were just unhappy folk who had wanted to be left alone and now found themselves having just killed over thirty pretty much defenceless people. Never mind that the Corps had been about to destroy their village, and those very solders would have done the same to them without a second thought; the Abbas folk stood there feeling like cowardly murderers. They found themselves unable to move even, as they collectively wondered, "What next?"

Eventually Dorcas spoke, "We'll need to get rid of these bodies before the children return… and then we're going to have to talk. A lot! Come on, let's get this sorted, friends, we can't stand here all day."

The ice was broken as they set about clearing up the mess and dragging the bodies away, digging a mass grave and burying them. But as the remaining members of the community returned, and the lookouts began going out again, the mood was bleak.

It was even bleaker amongst the magery team as they gathered that evening. None of them had individually killed a soldier, but each felt personally responsible for the deaths of so many. "It wasn't what I thought I had signed up for." said Luke. "I have been hankering all this time for a more impressive, powerful gift but, now I find I have it, I'm suddenly shocked by what I … what we … can do! " said Luke.

Iffley agreed, saying how different it had felt from repelling bears or throwing cats at each other.

"Couldn't we have simply Ported them away, like we did with the bears?" Tam asked.

"Possibly," replied Aldred, "but then they would have been able to come back in greater numbers… and with Mages too?"

"I agree," said Sharla, "but what worries me now is that we have started something that has consequences. That patrol going missing will be noticed, and more and bigger groups will come after them. Can we seriously expect to sit here and hope that won't happen?"

Luke remarked wryly that he'd always said that hiding was a pretty rubbish strategy, though he and the others realised that they actually had no alternative suggestions.

"We'll just have to wait and see what Dorcas and the Elders come up with," said Callan eventually. "She's pretty wise and has led us successfully for years. I'm sure she'll come up with something useful."

In the event there were no great innovations decided upon by the community meeting, other than a variation on their hiding policy. It was agreed that though they had survived the winter in Forest Abbas, it was an unsuitable place to settle in the long-term; the community agreed to return to their former location. If they were visited by Imperial Corps, they would pretend to be simply a rural village and feign no knowledge of their Forest Abbas. In future, Luke could make the magery team Unseen - and do so at a much earlier stage this time, so that even if the scouts brought a Seeker, they would not be revealed as having Mages amongst them. Hopefully the soldiers would simply go away again. Generally folk sounded unconvinced, but it was agreed, after much talking, as the least worst plan.

The packing started almost immediately and within days they were back on the road, returning to better accommodation, and, more comforting yet, away from the site of the recent slaughter. Aldred and the team were as unhappy as anyone else but, despite agreeing that there must be a better way, were likewise unable to come up with anything else.

So, with the same degree of reluctance as the rest of the populace, they set off on the return journey to Abbas.

23 RETURN TO ABBAS

By summer time, the community was feeling rather more optimistic, though Aldred and the team remained distinctly sceptical about the future. They had considered leaving the community, but eventually decided that the experience of living off the land as scavengers, in the way Aldred and the other two had, was just too hard to be a long-term option. Yet they couldn't work out a way of living openly in the Empire without ultimately their magery being discovered.

Certainly, though, the location was better able to support the folks, with their cottage gardens and fruit trees already reasonably established and able to provide food. They even considered ploughing up the land beyond the current boundaries to grow crops in due course to further advance their identity as a bone fide village and less as a hidden one.

Thus, when a group of the Imperial Corps eventually stumbled upon the village, they were greeted with a reasonably convincing mixture of innocence and suspicion, whilst the magery group made themselves suitably Unseen. After several more visits from other groups of scouts, even Aldred's group began to feel a bit more positive.

However, when another later group arrived, one of their number turned out to have been amongst the scouts who had discovered it the previous year, whilst Aldred had been hiding there. He wanted to know why it had been deserted? Dorcas' cover story, about an illness meaning they had all evacuated it and kept away for the winter, was obviously not believed.

Nevertheless months passed, the village prospered and everyone began to feel that, maybe there was a future. Might the plan, flawed as it was, possibly work?

Until that is, one day when Luke, Callan, Sharla and Marsha returned from a session they carried out periodically of long-distance far-seeing. They could scan together over the terrain miles away and had grown very familiar with settlements large and small and the usual numbers of people populating them. This survey, though, revealed not only a large variation in numbers in one town to the south, but, using Callan's skills, even more worrying information.

They called for Aldred to join them, incorporating his Seeker abilities and personal experience into their gestalt far-seeing and he confirmed their worst fears. "We need to talk with Dorcas," he said immediately. "She's meeting with the Elders and they need to know what we know!"

As the group walked in, Dorcas could tell by looking at Luke's pale face that they weren't coming with good news.

"We're in big trouble, I'm afraid," said Aldred. "There's a large army approaching from the south. Worse than that, our group picked up that there are powerful Mages amongst their number, and I have confirmed their identity."

He paused for a few seconds before dropping the bombshell nobody was expecting. "I'm afraid it's Camrin and Magrat! I can't think of any reason why they would leave the capital unless they thought there was a major threat to their existence, and the only thing I can envisage they might imagine to be such a threat, is us!"

Other faces in the room went the same shade as Luke's, and there was a deep silence in the room. Several times an Elder cleared his or her throat to say something, and then realised it wasn't worth saying. The only thought in everyone's mind was that the plan, the poor but so far successful plan, had finally unravelled, and they were in trouble. Real trouble.

Eventually they started to realistically look at the options. There weren't many of these, and mostly they were pretty limited! Once again they came to the conclusion that they were not a fighting community and were too small to lead a rebellion unaided. There was no great appetite to all hide and attack the army as before. No-one was convinced they could hide the whole village community from such powerful Mages as the Empress and Emperor, not to mention the massive amount of blood that would be spent was beyond imagination.

They had a few days to evacuate some of the more vulnerable and possibly offer some folks the chance to flee if they wanted to leave, but all in all the only option seemed to be to continue with their original plan: Hide the Mages and pretend.

This time Luke exploded, his face now bright red. "You can't mean that? Surely you can't believe it will work? It's madness and it cannot work! Not this time! There must, there must be another way?"

"Then find it, Luke," said an exhausted Dorcas, "because I'm damned if I can think of it!"

Luke turned and walked out, muttering, "Must be, must be!" and the room descended into silence and fear.

24 CONFRONTING THE EMPERORS

There were several days before the army and the Imperial rulers would arrive and, though a handful of folks did indeed decide to leave, the overwhelming majority of people had simply concluded that if this was the end of Abbas, then they felt resigned to face what was coming. They were tired of running, tired of living in the shadow of an evil Empire, convinced they didn't have the fight to oppose it or the energy so to do. They had survived by hiding; they were good at doing it, pretending to be normal, and it was the only plan they had. If there was some alternative, they couldn't think of it and they had simply had enough. They would face the future with heads held high.

When the lookouts announced that the Empire's forces were within sight, everybody set about looking as normal as possible, barely even looking up when the first heavily-armed soldiers entered the village. The magery team had been Unseen for some days, Luke having worked out a way some months back of maintaining this in conjunction with Marsha even while he slept, and they had withdrawn to the far parts of the village. They could, though, watch the proceedings from their vantage point.

The initial interactions went quite well, as the experience of demonstrating their deceptive normality kicked in. However, once the Emperor and his wife entered, the questions became harder and harder to answer. What had led them to live here on the margins of the Empire? Why had they vacated the village the year before? Where had they gone then? Had it been in the forests to the North west? Did thy know what had happened to a group of Imperial Corps who had disappeared there? Why were they clearly lying about their activities?

As the interrogation grew in intensity, Camrin's Melder and Magrat's Pather abilities began to be utilised, to force folk to tell the truth. Luke was deeply impressed by how strong Dorcas was in resisting the full force of the Imperial powers, but when the soldiers also started to beat the villagers, he pathed to the group:

> [*"I don't think I can stand this any more. Come on, let's go closer. I'm going to try something I've not tried before. Marsha and Sharla, I'm going to need as much augmentation as you can manage!"*
>
> *"Not sure this is the time for innovation, Luke!" pathed Aldred*
>
> *"Possibly, my friend, but maybe it's time we did something different?" he replied.*]

Aldred could see there was no way of changing the young man's mind as he had already set off towards the village centre before Aldred could stop him. He was also amazed to realise that as Luke walked into the middle of the action, he seemed to be being seen by those around him. Somehow he was visible, yet he had managed to maintain the rest of the magery team's in their Unseen status. That gave them some flexibility and freedom but he realised that if anything happened to Luke, their cover would disappear.

> [*"How have you done that, Luke? And why?"*
>
> *"I need to talk with them and I think what I'm about to do will only work if they don't know there are several of us!"*
>
> *"And what exactly, are you going to do, Luke? Don't you think we should have agreed this together?"*
>
> *"No, Aldred," pathed back Luke, "there's no time for discussions I'm afraid, This time it's going to be your turn to trust me! Now please, for all our sakes, shut up!"*]

Then, suddenly and grandly, Luke intoned, "Your Majesties, may I welcome you to Abbas and politely request that you leave these poor folk alone and stop your people hurting my friends!"

Clearly quite used to magery 'tricks,' the Emperor showed no surprise at Luke's sudden appearance and was clearly not going to admit to being impressed! "Why should I, Mr Invisible one moment and visible the next?" he sneered.

"If you won't then, I shall stop them," said Luke, at the same time waving his hands towards the soldiers (whilst simultaneously pathing instructions to Iffley to Port them away.)

The effect was dramatic and impressive: the whole front row of soldiers were thrown backwards and away from the villagers, crashing into their colleagues behind them, apparently as a result of Luke's actions.

Camrin responded by mimicking Luke's arm action, waving his own in the direction of a line of villagers, Porting them backwards violently. "Two can play at that game, child," he growled at Luke.

"Then do it to me, not to your loyal subjects, your Majesty!" taunted Luke.

The Emperor responded by focusing completely on Luke, and sent a massive wave of force at the young man, fully expecting his body to fly off into the distance.

To Camrin's amazement - indeed, that of the Empress and the whole cortege - absolutely nothing happened to Luke, apart from a slight backwards swaying.

He was of course unaware that Luke was not alone but was in constant pathic communication with the group, so much faster than verbal speech. The months of team-building and working together had come to fruition at last; vast amounts happening and yet somehow everything seemed in slow motion. As Camrin had sent his Porting wave, Luke had calmly called the team to hold, support and augment his shielding against the onslaught, at the same time asking them to warn him of whatever else might be to come.

Following Camrin's initial attack came several more blasts, each stronger than its predecessor.

["Pathic and Melding blasts coming too." sent Callan]

The warning arrived as Magrat joined in her husband's attack, sending deep, penetrating waves of mental commands and undermining thoughts. Under such a dual but separate onslaught, any normal Mage, even a massively powerful one, would probably have buckled. But again, united mentally with the team, Luke stood passively and apparently unaffected.

In actual fact he was beginning to feel the strain of repelling the mental attacks but unexpectedly he found the period as Dung Man had served him well. Those months of being excluded from and reviled by his community had taught him the ability to appear calm and entirely unbothered. He had developed what in a past age had been known as a 'poker face' and he exhibited it effectively, enraging the two Mages who redoubled their efforts, which were equally ineffective.

Camrin changed tack and ordered their soldiers forward to add to the attack.

["Porting now" pathed Iffley]

Luke apparently easily swept them back with a casual wave of his arm, and smiled grimly. This was working better than he had hoped. Indeed, as the group worked together, their battling became surprisingly easier to carry out! Spears and arrows fired at him simply stopped mid-air, just as both Magrat and Camrin took in a huge breath, ready to launch a yet greater attack.

But in the second before they did, Luke simply said, "Your Majesties …"

They hesitated and he continued, "Your Majesties, this is a little tedious. Why do we not simply talk awhile?"

"Why should we talk with a scruffy, common scum-child like you?" sneered the Emperor.

"For a start, because for the first time in your lives you have met someone who can stand up to your vile power. And secondly because you may have noticed that so far I have responded to your attacks with nothing but defensive shielding. I am clearly immune to what you can throw at me, and yet, vulnerable as you are, or seem to be, I have yet to unleash any offensive powers in response. Have you perhaps wondered why that might be?"

"Perhaps you have none!" snorted an equally sneering Magrat.

"I suppose that is possible, but perhaps you should look down for a second?" smiled Luke as the ruling monarchs of the great Empire of the new age momentarily glanced downwards, to find that over the last moments had each slowly been elevated a foot or so above the ground. For the first time, they looked slightly shocked, as, equally gently, they were lowered slowly to the ground again.

["Nice one, team!" pathed Luke.]

"Do you not think that someone who can levitate you, without you even noticing might just be able to do something more destructive?" Luke asked, gently. "So how about we talk for just a bit? Then, perhaps we can decide what we do next."

"We have nothing to say to you, despite your party tricks," said Magrat, though demonstrating a little doubt in her voice as she replied.

"Well maybe you should just listen to what I have to say, instead?" said Luke. By this time he was beginning to feel the strain of maintaining the group being Unseen in addition to maintaining pathic and verbal communications, whilst equally maintaining his air of equanimity. To his relief, just at that moment, almost as if they knew his growing weakness, he realised that the team had walked forwards and formed a ring, with him at the front. Even more encouraging, he found Marsha was now standing next to him and firmly taking his hand. She remained Unseen to all but the magery team.

["Keep going, you're doing great. I've no idea what you're up to but keep it up!" she pathed.

"I said there must be a better way, and I think I've worked out what it is."

"That's good, Luke. I believe in you and I trust you!" she replied.]

Re-energised, Luke continued. "I don't know why you have come all this way from the capital your Majesties, but I suspect you may have caught on that somewhere around here there was a group who were not completely under your control and your power. And somehow you were threatened by such a thing, which from your viewpoint I can understand. You have used strength and force to gain your position, so you naturally expect that anyone who has magery gifts would behave likewise,

Camrin laughed scornfully, "So says the leader of a group who slaughtered a group of my Imperial Corps in the forest and buried them in a mass grave! It sounds like strength and force are games you play, too!"

"Ah, I wondered if you had found them! Yes that was us, but we were forced into defending ourselves, and deeply regret the effect of our response. We vowed we would not do things that way any more. Because that is your outlook and your way and not ours.

"So, I ask you again, have you in any way been threatened by me and the community here? Indeed did any of those poor Mages you have ripped away from their homes over the years offer any threat at all before you disposed of them? I suspect not!

"You have been blessed with massive gifts and abilities yet what, actually have you achieved with them?"

"How dare you ask, you impertinent piece of filth? What gives you the right to ask such a thing of us, the most powerful Mage-Emperor and Empress of the New Age?" responded Camrin.

"The same rights you have denied your subjects for too long. The right to free expression, the right to be treated as people, the right to make our own futures, rather than being dependant on the whims of people of power. People who take what they want, and give nothing in return!"

"You are our subjects and we do not grant you such rights, boy!"

"Perhaps, your Majesty, you might consider us as citizens, not subjects, and give it a go? And while you consider that proposal, let me tell you a story ..."

"We have no need for stories, child!" snorted Magrat.

"Oh, I rather think you do, Majesty," responded Luke, firmly. "You will recall you once had a Seeker called Aldred?"

"Indeed, the disloyal scoundrel. Still on the run, no doubt!"

"The reason he left your service was that he met and fell in love with someone. They had a child who grew up with magery gifts, so he protected her and fled to stop your reign of terror killing his child. Your Majesties, I would suggest that's not disloyalty. Rather, that is love. Is it not true that you, too, have a child? Would you also not make sacrifices for him?"

"You're out of date, boy. Our son grew sickly and weak and died a year ago. A shame, but if he wasn't strong enough to reach adulthood ..." the Emperor began, but was interrupted by Magrat.

"We don't need to share our story with this common vermin, husband!" Turning back to Luke, she said, "And as for that traitor Aldred, he was planning a coup. He planned to use his daughter's power to overthrow us. His actions had nothing to do with love!"

"Not true, your Imperial Majesty. Not true at all! You have no evidence for your fears except how you think others might behave, based upon what you yourselves would do. And that is your weakness!"

Cursing suddenly and wildly about not being weak, Camrin sent another powerful wave of Porting power at Luke.

But Luke was ready for it. Though it slightly winded him, he grinned broadly and said, "More weakness, your Majesty?"

["Don't goad him too much, Luke!" pathed Aldred through the group, "We don't know how powerful your augmented ability to absorb attacks are."

"Yeah, ok, but I think I'm getting through," replied Luke. "Hold on and keep your eyes open for any more sudden blasts, please?]

121

To the Imperial couple, he continued, "But you do have strengths too, and you could use them better. That's all I am saying. You see, I have been studying a book which has taught me much."

"Books? We banned them! They're full of the cursedness of the past so-called 'Great Age.' Full of wickedness and foolishness. No wonder you think you can stand up against us ..."

"Ah, but full, too, of wisdom and great ideas. For instance one teacher in my favourite book talked of doing to others what you would wish them to do to you. Oh yes, and loving your neighbour as much as you love yourself. That's not foolishness, that's a brilliant way to be!"

"What are you talking about, you stupid infant?"

Luke hesitated, despite the encouragement from Marsha's hand gripping his.

["Make me visible, Luke," pathed Marsha, "I think I can add to your arguments?"

"Are you sure?"

"Dare I say , 'Trust me'?"]

Luke nodded and Marsha duly appeared beside Luke. Strangely, this couple of young people from a Forgetter community, habitually used to hiding, somehow appeared more regal and assured than the increasingly perplexed royal couple before them. Never before had anyone been able either to stand up to their power, or to have the courage to talk back to them. And Mages appearing out of thin air was beginning to disconcert them, too.

"Your Majesties," said Marsha, "Luke and I grew up in a community outside your Empire, where everybody looked after everybody else, from the weakest to the strongest. From the older to the younger ones, too. It wasn't perfect, but we cared for each other and ensured we all had a role and a possibility to offer what we had to the community. They fled from this world of hate, fear and mistrust to find a better way."

"Meanwhile," Luke continued, "the Empire you have developed has gone the other way, creating a society run by the powerful for the powerful. People simply tread on the weakest as if they mean nothing!"

Magrat sneered, "But they don't mean anything. They live to serve us. They love to serve us!"

"Which is why so many of them are starving and struggling to live?" said Luke. "They don't love you, your Majesties! The truth is that they hate you, and couldn't wait to get you back if only they were able! Just think, if you had ruled with love, they might truly love you in return!"

Marsha added, "Not only that, you wouldn't have to look behind you everywhere you went in fear that someone was behind you ready to stab you in the back! You wouldn't have to send your Seekers to slaughter anyone with gifts in case they threatened you. And you wouldn't need to send your bully boys to steal food from your subjects!"

Their words, however, were not breaking through. The emperor forced a laugh and issued a challenge. "Then try it yourself, boy! We're bored of you now, with your silly party tricks. Come on, stop wasting time with talks and stupid children's stories. Hit us with your worst! We are tired of your nonsense!"

Luke and Marsha looked at each other and nodded simultaneously. "That's a shame, and I have to say I am disappointed, So … OK, your Majesties," said Luke, "here it comes."

["What are we doing?" asked Iffley.

"Nothing! Do you remember that story on the mountain top? The real power wasn't in the earthquake, fire or wind but in the still small voice of silence. I've just realised that my gifts aren't about power and that love is greater than hate!"

"This isn't a time for philosophy, Luke! This is serious!" pathed Aldred

"Just wait!" Luke replied. "I am deadly serious, I can assure you!]

Luke paused for a second or two, which seemed like hours, then simply raised his arms above his head and gently said, "Emperor Camrin and Empress Magrat, I hereby forgive you."

"You what?" they both exclaimed.

"I forgive you! You didn't know what you were doing. You didn't realise the harm you were inflicting on those you ruled. So, on behalf of the whole Empire, I forgive you. Forgiveness is the most powerful weapon in the world and I give you it with a generous and loving heart. Now go and do likewise to your Empire!"

Luke's greatest hope was that his words would heal these powerful Mages and turn them away from cruelty and towards love, but he was not expecting it to happen.

["Be ready, team." he pathed quickly, "This one will be their biggest and their best. We need to be bigger and better."]

Magrat and Camrin looked at each other briefly and then, just as Luke had sadly expected, the two mighty Mages hit Luke with a wave of force such as the world had not seen since the Mage Wars of the past. Flames, wind and flashes of light emanated from their arms as they sent every ounce of their vitriol, hatred, power, force and coercion at the young irritants before them, emptying out everything they could throw at them.

Luke and Marsha linked arms and opened their outer arms wide, as if in acceptance and embrace of all that was being thrown at them. They were beginning to feel incredibly weary, but their faces were smiling broadly, which made the royal attack even more ferocious.

And yet, still the team held firm, as Luke and Marsha continued to brace themselves against the forces hurled against them, for what seemed an age. Luke was grateful once again for Marsha's physical hold, in addition to the augmentation that she sent, though worryingly he could feel even this was beginning to wane.

He could sense though, that the power of the onslaught being thrown from the royal couple was also gradually failing until, eventually it just petered out.

Luke dropped to his knees and then looked up to see his adversaries were likewise collapsing, never having before expended so much, and never before finding themselves not victorious.

He took a deep breath and checked something with Aldred.

[*"Can you feel what I can feel?" he asked.*

"What do you mean?"

"It sort of feels as if their magery has wained. Like the burning out in mages battles of the Mage War, you once told me about! You're a Seeker - Seek them now please? What can you sense?"

"By golly, I think you're right, Luke! There's nothing there. No magery, no power, no... no ..."

"No gifts, I think you mean!" pathed Luke, smiling once again in relief.]

He stood up and walked over to the couple, who looked suddenly aged and broken, and offered a hand up. "Your Majesties, your magery is gone. You have burnt yourselves out trying to destroy, us and in the process have destroyed yourselves."

"No!" shouted a suddenly re-enraged Camrin jumping up. Having first tried and failed to send another wave of Porting power at Luke, he drew his ceremonial sword to deal with his vanquisher the old fashioned way. Luke, though simply stepped back as the sword was whipped out of the ruler's hand and flew to the ground.

"Attack them! Kill them!" shouted Magrat, but without any effect upon the soldiers. Instead, the Commander with his red feathered helmet took a few steps forwards. "Are you telling me that he has no magery power left?" he asked Luke.

"So it seems!"

"In that case," responded the Commander of the Corps, "having witnessed what we have just seen, he is no longer the one we follow. Under the ways of the Empire I acknowledge you as my ruler!" And with that, he knelt down and dropped his head, placed his fist across his chest and said, "Hail, Emperor Luke!" All around the village, his soldiers did likewise.

Luke smiled and said, "Commander, stand up and let me tell you another story. Once upon a time there was a young man who learnt he had magery gifts, and thought they were about power. The past two years have taught him, rather, that real power is about doing good. To do the right thing. He hasn't defeated the Emperor to become his replacement. He has learnt that there is a better way than the ways of the Empire. This is the end of those ways. This is ..."

[*"Watch out, Luke!" pathed Sharla.*]

For during this conversation Camrin had crept over, retrieved his sword and suddenly ran towards Luke, lunging wildly at him. He almost certainly would have achieved his aim if the Commander, a trained and experienced soldier, hadn't swiftly drawn his own sword and coldly stabbed his Emperor in the heart. There was a moment of sheer silence across Abbas as Camrin clutched his chest, looked at his blood-stained hands and dropped dead.

The Commander looked around dispassionately and then asked, "There may be a better way and a better future, sir, of that I am uncertain. What I do know is that it will be better without him. Should I do likewise to her, I wonder?"

At this, Magrat rolled over into a foetal position and began to weep.

"Do you remember that teacher I told the Emperor about, Commander? One of his other sayings was something about turning the other cheek. I tried to do that with the two of them when I said I forgave them. Indeed it was what my friends and I were doing the whole time just now: jointly turning our cheeks to the Imperial onslaught." As he said this he indicated the group around him, and the soldier realised that they had now been visible for some time, though quite when they had appeared he wasn't sure.

"I'm beginning to believe that cheek-turning is the most powerful weapon in the world," said Luke firmly. "I'm just sad I couldn't teach it to Camrin!"

"I am a soldier, sir," replied the Commander, "and such a theory is beyond my experience. It would take much to convince me it is so."

"Possibly the teacher I mentioned might do so, Commander. Perhaps if we shared his wisdom with you, we might persuade you in time!" laughed Luke, delightfully relieved but desperately weary.

"For now," said Marsha, "let us offer you and your soldiers, not to mention this poor weary widow here, a rest from your travels and a meal."

25 A NEW BEGINNING

The next days were confusing and disorientating. The Abbas folk reestablished their routines whilst also offering hospitality to the soldiers who, freed from their command structure, took some time to work out what to do next. Some of the more recently recruited Corps members negotiated with their Commander that they should be released to return to their own villages, once it became clear that Luke was adamant that he would not be returning to the capital with them.

Freed from their Imperial command, the soldiers did seem overall a pretty decent bunch. Nevertheless there was a high level of relief when they eventually moved on, especially as they took with them the former Empress, now completely broken. There was some doubt if she would survive the journey but the transformation from feeling fear for her to pity wasn't easy.

"Now we need to plan for the future too, friends!" announced Dorcas. "We are even shorter of food supplies after our guests' stay with us and perhaps we need to decide whether we actually need to stay here, now that the danger we were fleeing from has been removed. The general mood was agreement, although there was also a concern, for all Luke's optimism that with the source of the evil in the Empire removed, there would be a better, fairer society in its place.

"We are all 'Children of Camrin and Magrat,' and their influence will continue for some time, I suspect." Aldred commented. "People are used to power being the way things are sorted out, and minor Mages and armed solders may decide their time has come to try to flex their own muscles."

"And I used to call you an idealist, Aldred!" laughed Marsha.

Others suggested that, since Luke had such a vision and belief, he ought to have taken up the role offered by the Commander in order to implement it. Luke, however, replied that he believed that once people got used to governing by power and force alone, they could easily slip into tyranny. In any case, the defeat of the Empire had been achieved not by his own power but by that of the team, working together. In actual fact he had virtually no gift of his own anyway, apart from his own passive ones. He had of course not told the Corps Commander that!

There was also, now the Corps had left, something else he had to share, which he had not revealed while they were still there.

"It wasn't just Camrin and Magrat who were burnt out and reduced by the conflict of magery. Working together, augmented by Marsha and Sharla, we were able to resist their attacks and allow them to burn magery out of their systems in their fury.

"However, in the process of doing so, it seems that we, too have been massively drained of our gifts. Our Pathic bond remains in place, but we have mostly been reduced to near normality. Iffley and Sharla can barely Port a pebble, even together, and the augmentation skills of Sharla and Marsha are greatly diminished. If Camrin's sword had been much bigger, we would not have been able to disarm him. Truth is, we got a bit lucky there!"

"If that Commander had realised that," added Aldred, "I suspect your fate would've been the same as his former Emperor, Luke. So well done on not sharing with him! My feeling is that I know a lot of folks - good folks - back at the capital. Perhaps I could work with them to see if we could sort out a better way of running things, as Luke suggests? What you do as a community is up to you, but Mahanda, Sharla, Iffley and I have decided to return home."

Some others said likewise that, now the reason they had left their villages had been removed, they also intended to return to them. Others yet felt that the community that had been formed in Abbas was better than what they had left and, after all it was a functioning and sustainable village, so they felt happy to remain. After some discussions about the details, the meeting began to draw to a close.

Callan, however added that he and Portha had also decided to stay. He also asked whether the folk who would be leaving might delay their departure for a short time to enjoy a celebration, as he and his betrothed became formally married? Tam and Arkan took the opportunity to announce what most had guessed already, that they, too were a couple and would like it to be formally acknowledged too. Sharla proposed that there should be a double wedding and the room burst out with whoops and cheers! The meeting ended on a high note with everyone leaving with smiles on their faces and optimism in the air.

Romance wasn't only evident on the debating floor, though. Luke, who had been sitting next to Marsha throughout the discussions, slowly reached out his hand and, for the first time since the conflagration they had both faced from the Imperial pair, gently took hers in his again.

"You've taken a long time to do that," she responded, smiling and looking into his eyes.

"Well, perhaps I just had to find out who I actually am, before I could gather the courage to think about being more than that?"

She dropped her eyes gently, then asked "And would you like to be more than just you?"

"Oh I think so! How about you?"

She squeezed his hand back and smiled again. "We have learnt a lot since our days in Coldharbour, and mostly about the power of working together. I think I'd rather enjoy continuing that learning experience."

"Good," he said, leaning forwards and kissing her lips for a delicious and eternal moment.

When their lips parted, he added, "Mentioning Coldharbour, there's something else I was going to say about it. We did say originally our aim was to return and make things better there and…"

"Later," she said, "I think there's some more overdue kissing to do first?"

THE END

ENDNOTE

Many months has passed in preparation and travel and the wind was blowing strongly as the boat approached the Cleft Rock. Luke thought wryly to himself that it was not as strong as it had been on that last, fateful time when he had sailed towards it.

More significantly, then, he had been alone.

This time he was, happily, accompanied.

A final change was that his Feeling was there, but markedly reduced and a part of him grieved that loss.

On the other hand, he was confident that, together, they would more than compensate as the two of them closed their eyes, melded their minds together and jointly sunk their united consciousness deeply into their boat and down into the sea, to sense the coming of the Surge. With confirmation they prepared to turn inland.

"I suppose we ought to look backwards, in case there's any Outlanders following us?" teased Marsha.

"We're the Outlanders these days!" he riposted, but almost instinctively did indeed look over his shoulder to view the thankfully empty seas. "Ready?" he asked.

"As I'll ever be." she replied

"Ok. Hey, do you want to steer?" he offered to her, and even to his own surprise.

"Oh you have grown up, my love!" she laughed delightedly. "Perhaps, though we could do it together?"

And so, united in mind and to a degree in body too, they jointly grasped the tiller and turned the boat towards the still hidden entrance to Coldharbour.

After their combined efforts and Feeling had successfully guided them through the curves of the channel (as they had somehow navigated them in their battles for survival and against the powerful Empire), they stowed the sails and steered themselves on the momentum of the Surge towards the shores of the village. There, already, they had been spotted and a crowd was collecting.

A crowd who would appreciate the stores of metals, tools and exotic foods to delight their palates. Whether they themselves would be welcomed was still slightly in some doubt, but, as Luke proudly stroked his partner's now slightly bulging belly, he hoped their announcement of a new Coldharbour child on the way, together with the news that the Outland was a better, safer place, would overcome the fears their arrival would inevitably engender.

He leant over the tiller and kissed her one more time and asked, "Ready for this, Marsha?"

She happily, kissed him back, and said, once again, "As I'll ever be."

The Beginning

GLOSSARY

Abbas	Village hideout of Sharla and the Resistance
Aldred	Outlander and Seeker
Aloric	Coldharbour maiden - surprisingly Feeled
Arkan	Abbas villager & Pather
Arlaf	Elder of Coldharbour and father to Luke
Bharak	Abbas villager
Brusca	Father of Portha, Abbas blacksmith
Callan	Villager outcast by Abbas folk following unfounded accusations & Pather
Camrin	Emperor - both Melder and Porter
Central Stream	One of three small rivers running through Coldharbour - used for washing and bathing rather than drinking water.
Cleft Rock	Landmark by which Fishers identify entry to Coldharbour
Coldharbour	Hidden Village - home of Marsha and Luke
Dorcas	Village Chief Elder of Abbas
Ellen	Offwell villager
Gineering	Engineering
Great Age	Era before the Great Disaster and catastrophic climatic changes
Feeling	Mage ability to sense the sea tides … and more!

Forgetters	Those who fled the Mage Wars bad sought to escape further by suppressing memories and remembering of the past.
Iffley	Abbas villager & Porter
Islands (The)	Archipelago to the west of Southfleet making up the third Kingdom of the current Age
Luke	Fisher of Coldharbour, strong in Feeling
Magrat	Empress - both Pather and Seeker
Mahanda	Aldred's wife and Sharla's mother
Marsha	Coldharbour maiden - surprisingly Feeled
Melders	Mages with the power to control the minds of other people
Mersheens	Machines of the Great Age
Offwell	Village to the south west of Abbas
Porters	Mages with the power to move objects
Portha	Abbas village girl
Pathers	Mages with telepathic power to read the emotions and minds of other people
Ruark	Kingdom of the current Age in the mountainous northerly regions of the land
Syence	Science
Seeker	Mages with the ability to discern magery and discriminate between gifts

Sharla	Child rescued by Aldred & Porter
Southfleet	Kingdom of the current Age in the central and southerly plains of the land
Spires	Twin rocks marking the exit from Coldharbour crater
Tam	Abbas villager & Pather
Teck	Technology

ABOUT THE AUTHOR

Peter Clark has had two careers - one in the National Health Service (he once was allowed to put RGN after his name) and one of equal length as a United Reformed Church Minister, working in Kent and then Dorset (so is allowed to put Rev'd before his name!)

He has now retired and has finally found the time to write the novel he has always said was within him. He hopes you like it.

He lives in West Dorset with his wife Susan - the artist who produced the beautiful felted artwork on the cover.

Printed in Great Britain
by Amazon

85864787R00079